"This exciting story is set in the last quarter of this century, but the action takes place in several levels of time and periods of history. A young convicted criminal becomes a volunteer in a government program which trains men to do research in these various areas. Object: the discovery of scientific secrets lost before the dawn of history."

—*Saturday Review*

"Well plotted, full of suspense, with many provocative concepts. Recommended."

—*Library Journal*

THE TIME TRADERS

ANDRE NORTON

SF
ace books
A Division of Charter Communications Inc.
A GROSSET & DUNLAP COMPANY
51 Madison Avenue
New York, New York 10010

THE TIME TRADERS

An ACE Book
by arrangement with The World Publishing Co.

This Ace printing: July 1980

4 6 8 0 9 7 5 3
Manufactured in the United States of America

1

TO ANYONE who glanced casually inside the detention room the young man sitting there did not seem very formidable. In height he might have been a little above average, but not enough to make him noticeable. His brown hair was cropped conservatively; his unlined boy's face was not one to be remembered—unless one was observant enough to note those light-gray eyes and catch a chilling, measuring expression showing now and then for an instant in their depths.

Neatly and inconspicuously dressed, in this last quarter of the twentieth century his like was to be found on any street of the city ten floors below—to all outward appearances. But that other person under the protective coloring so assiduously cultivated could touch heights of encased and controlled fury which Murdock himself did not understand and was only just learning to use as a weapon against a world he had always found hostile.

He was aware, though he gave no sign of it, that a guard was watching him. The cop on duty was an old hand—he probably expected some reaction other than passive acceptance from the prisoner. But he was not going to get it. The law had Ross sewed up tight this time. Why didn't they get about the business of shipping him off? Why had he had that afternoon session with the skull thumper? Ross had been on the defensive then, and he had not liked it. He had given to the other's questions all the attention his shrewd mind could muster, but a faint, very faint, apprehension still clung to the memory of that meeting.

The door of the detention room opened. Ross did not turn his head, but the guard cleared his throat as if their hour of mutual silence had dried his vocal cords. "On your feet, Murdock! The judge wants to see you."

Ross rose smoothly, with every muscle under fluid control. It never paid to talk back, to allow any sign of defiance to show. He would go through the motions as if he were a bad little boy who had realized his errors. It was a meek-and-mild act that had paid off more than once in Ross's checkered past. So he faced the man seated behind the desk in the other room with an uncertain, diffident smile, standing with boyish awkwardness, respectfully waiting for the other to speak first. Judge Ord Rawle. It was his rotten luck to pull old Eagle Beak on his case. Well, he would simply have to take it when the old boy dished it out. Not that he had to remain stuck with it later . . .

"You have a bad record, young man."

Ross allowed his smile to fade; his shoulders slumped. But under concealing lids his eyes showed an instant of cold defiance.

"Yes, sir," he agreed in a voice carefully cultivated to shake convincingly about the edges. Then suddenly all Ross's pleasure in the skill of his act was wiped away. Judge Rawle was not alone; that blasted skull thumper was sitting there, watching the prisoner with the same keenness he had shown the other day.

"A very bad record for the few years you have had to make it." Eagle Beak was staring at him, too, but without the same look of penetration, luckily for Ross. "By rights, you should be turned over to the new Rehabilitation Service . . ."

Ross froze inside. That was the "treatment," icy rumors of which had spread throughout his particular world. For the second time since he had entered the room his self-confidence was jarred. Then he clung with a degree of hope to the phrasing of that last sentence.

"Instead, I have been authorized to offer you a choice, Murdock. One which I shall state—and on record—I do not in the least approve."

Ross's twinge of fear faded. If the judge didn't like it, there must be something in it to the advantage of Ross Murdock. He'd grab it for sure!

"There is a government project in need of volunteers. It seems that you have tested out as possible material for this assignment. If you sign for it, the law will consider the time spent on it as part of your sentence. Thus you may aid the country which you have heretofore disgraced—"

"And if I refuse, I go to this rehabilitation. Is that right, sir?"

"I certainly consider you a fit candidate for rehabilitation. Your record—" He shuffled through the papers on his desk.

"I choose to volunteer for the project, sir."

The judge snorted and pushed all the papers into a folder. He spoke to a man waiting in the shadows.

"Here then is your volunteer, Major."

Ross bottled in his relief. He was over the first hump. And since his luck had held so far, he might be about to win all the way . . .

The man Judge Rawle called "Major" moved into the light. At the first glance Ross, to his hidden annoyance, found himself uneasy. To face up to Eagle Beak was all part of the game. But somehow he sensed one did not play such games with this man.

"Thank you, your honor. We will be on our way at once. This weather is not very promising."

Before he realized what was happening, Ross found himself walking meekly to the door. He considered trying to give the major the slip when they left the building, losing himself in a storm-darkened city. But they did not take the elevator downstairs. Instead, they climbed two or three flights up the emergency stairs. And to his humiliation Ross found himself panting and slowing, while the other man, who must have been a good dozen years his senior, showed no signs of discomfort.

They came out into the snow on the roof, and the major flashed a torch skyward, guiding in a dark shadow which touched down before them. A helicopter! For the first time Ross began to doubt the wisdom of his choice.

"On your way, Murdock!" The voice was impersonal enough, but that very impersonality got under one's skin.

Bundled into the machine between the silent major and an equally quiet pilot in uniform, Ross was lifted over the city, whose ways he knew as well as he knew the lines on his own palm, into the unknown he was already beginning to regard dubiously. The lighted streets and buildings, their outlines softened by the soft wet snow, fell out of sight. Now they could mark the outer highways. Ross refused to ask any questions. He could take this silent treatment, he *had* taken a lot of tougher things in the past.

The patches of light disappeared, and the country opened out. The plane banked. Ross, with all the familiar landmarks of his world gone, could not have said if they were headed north or south. But moments later not even the thick curtain of snowflakes could blot out the pattern of red lights on the ground, and the helicopter settled down.

"Come on!"

For the second time Ross obeyed. He stood shivering, engulfed in a miniature blizzard. His clothing, protection enough in the city, did little good against the push of the wind. A hand gripped his upper arm, and he was drawn forward to a low building. A door banged and Ross and his companion came into a region of light and very welcome heat.

"Sit down—over there!"

Too bewildered to resent orders, Ross sat. There were other men in the room. One, wearing a queer suit of padded clothing, a bulbous headgear hooked over his arm, was reading a paper. The major crossed to speak to him and after they conferred for a moment, the major beckoned Ross with a crooked finger. Ross trailed the officer into an inner room lined with lockers.

From one of the lockers the major pulled a suit like the pilot's, and began to measure it against Ross. "All right," he snapped. "Climb into this! We haven't all night."

Ross climbed into the suit. As soon as he fastened the last zipper his companion jammed one of the domed helmets on his head. The pilot looked in the door. "We'd better scramble, Kelgarries, or we may be grounded for the duration!"

They hurried back to the flying field. If the helicopter had been a surprising mode of travel, this new machine was something straight out of the future—a needle-slim ship poised on fins, its sharp nose lifting vertically into the heavens. There was a scaffolding along one side, which the pilot scaled to enter the ship.

Unwillingly, Ross climbed the same ladder and found that he must wedge himself in on his back, his knees hunched up almost under his chin. To make it worse, cramped as those quarters were, he had to share them with the major. A transparent hood snapped down and was secured, sealing them in.

During his short lifetime Ross had often been afraid, bitterly afraid. He had fought to toughen his mind and body against such fears. But what he experienced now was no ordinary fear; it was panic so strong that it made him feel sick. To be shut in this small place with the knowledge that he had no control over his immediate future brought him face to face with every terror he had ever known, all of them combined into one horrible whole.

How long does a nightmare last? A moment? An hour? Ross could not time his. But at last the weight of a giant hand clamped down on his chest, and he fought for breath until the world exploded about him.

He came back to consciousness slowly. For a second he thought he was blind. Then he began to sort out one shade of grayish light from another. Finally, Ross became aware that he no longer rested on his back, but was slumped in a seat. The world about him was wrung with a vibration that beat in turn through his body.

Ross Murdock had remained at liberty as long as he had because he was able to analyze a situation quickly. Seldom in the past five years had he been at a loss to deal with any challenging person or action. Now he was aware that he was on the defensive and was being kept there. He stared into the dark and thought hard and furiously. He was convinced that everything that was happening to him this day was designed with only one end in view—to shake his self-confidence and make him pliable. Why?

Ross had an enduring belief in his own abilities and he also possessed a kind of shrewd understanding seldom granted to one so young. He knew that while Murdock was important to Murdock, he was none too important in the scheme of things as a whole. He had a record—a record so bad that Rawle might easily have thrown the book at him. But it differed in one important way from that of many of his fellows; until now he had been able to beat most of the raps. Ross believed this was largely because he had always worked alone and taken pains to plan a job in advance.

Why now had Ross Murdock become so important to someone that they would do all this to shake him? He was a volunteer—for what? To be a guinea pig for some bug they wanted to learn how to kill cheaply and easily? They'd been in a big hurry to push him off base. Using the silent treatment, this rushing around in planes, they were really working to keep him groggy. So, all right, he'd give them a groggy boy all set up for their job, whatever it was. Only, was his act good enough to fool the major? Ross had a hunch that it might not be, and that really hurt.

It was deep night now. Either they had flown out of the path of the storm or were above it. There were stars shining through the cover of the cockpit, but no moon.

Ross's formal education was sketchy, but in his own fashion he had acquired a range of knowledge which would have surprised many of the authorities who had had to deal with him. All the wealth of a big city library had been his to explore, and he had spent much time there, soaking up facts in many odd branches of learning. Facts were very useful things. On at least three occasions assorted scraps of knowledge had preserved Ross's freedom, once, perhaps his life.

Now he tried to fit together the scattered facts he knew about his present situation into some proper pattern. He was inside some new type of super-super atomjet, a machine so advanced in design that it would not have been used for anything that was not an important mission. Which meant that Ross Murdock had become necessary to someone, somewhere. Knowing that fact should give him a slight edge in the future, and he might well need such an edge. He'd just have to wait, play dumb, and use his eyes and ears.

At the rate they were shooting along they ought to be out of the country in a couple of hours. Didn't the Government have bases over half the world to keep the "cold peace"? Well, there was nothing for it. To be planted abroad someplace might interfere with plans for escape, but he'd handle that detail when he was forced to face it.

Then suddenly Ross was on his back once more, the giant hand digging into his chest and middle. This time there were no lights on the ground to guide them in. Ross had no intimation that they had reached their destination until they set down with a jar which snapped his teeth together.

The major wriggled out, and Ross was able to stretch his cramped body. But the other's hand was already on his shoulder, urging him along. Ross crawled free and clung dizzily to a ladderlike disembarking structure.

Below there were no lights, only an expanse of open snow. Men were moving across that blank area, gathering at the foot of the ladder. Ross was hungry and very tired. If the major wanted to play games, he hoped that such action could wait until the next morning.

In the meantime he must learn where "here" was. If he had a chance to run, he wanted to know the surrounding territory. But that hand was on his arm, drawing him along toward a door that stood half-open. As far as Ross could see, it led to the interior of a hillock of snow. Either the storm or men had done a very good cover-up job, and somehow Ross knew the camouflage was intentional.

That was Ross's introduction to the base, and after his arrival his view of the installation was extremely limited. One day was spent in undergoing the most searching physical he had ever experienced. And after the doctors had poked and pried he was faced by a series of other tests no one bothered to explain. Thereafter he was introduced to solitary, that is, confined to his own company in a cell-like room with a bunk that was more comfortable than it looked and an announcer in a corner of the ceiling. So far he had been told exactly nothing. And so far he had asked no questions, stubbornly keeping up his end of what he believed to be a tug of wills. At the moment, safely alone and lying flat on his bunk he eyed the announcer, a very dangerous young man and one who refused to yield an inch.

"Now hear this . . ." The voice transmitted

through that grill was metallic, but its rasp held overtones of Kelgarries' voice. Ross's lips tightened. He had explored every inch of the walls and knew that there was no trace of the door which had admitted him. With only his bare hands to work with he could not break out, and his only clothes were the shirt, sturdy slacks, and a pair of soft-soled moccasins that they had given him.

". . . to identity . . ." droned the voice. Ross realized that he must have missed something, not that it mattered. He was almost determined not to play along any more.

There was a click, signifying that Kelgarries was through braying. But the customary silence did not close in again. Instead, Ross heard a clear, sweet trilling which he vaguely associated with a bird. His acquaintance with all feathered life was limited to city sparrows and plump park pigeons, neither of which raised their voices in song, but surely those sounds were bird notes. Ross glanced from the mike in the ceiling to the opposite wall and what he saw there made him sit up, with the instant response of an alerted fighter.

For the wall was no longer there! Instead, there was a sharp slope of ground cutting down from peaks where the dark green of fir trees ran close to the snow line. Patches of snow clung to the earth in sheltered places, and the scent of those pines was in Ross's nostrils, real as the wind touching him with its chill.

He shivered as a howl sounded loudly and echoed, bearing the age-old warning of a wolf pack, hungry and a-hunt. Ross had never heard that sound before, but his human heritage subconsciously recognized it for what it was—death on four feet. Similarly, he was able to identify the gray shadows slinking about the nearest trees, and his hands balled into fists as he looked wildly about him for some weapon.

The bunk was under him and three of the four walls of the room enclosed him like a cave. But one of those gray skulkers had raised its head and was looking directly at him, its redish eyes alight. Ross ripped the top blanket off the bunk with a half-formed idea of snapping it at the animal when it sprang.

Stiff-legged, the beast advanced, a gutteral growl sounding deep in its throat. To Ross the animal, larger than any dog he had ever seen and twice as vicious, was a monster. He had the blanket ready before he realized that the wolf was not watching him after all, and that its attention was focused on a point out of his line of vision.

The wolf's muzzle wrinkled in a snarl, revealing long yellow-white teeth. There was a singing twang, and the animal leaped into the air, fell back, and rolled on the ground, biting despairingly at a shaft protruding from just behind its ribs. It howled again, and blood broke from its mouth.

Ross was beyond surprise now. He pulled himself together and got up, to walk steadily toward the dying wolf. And he wasn't in the least amazed when his outstretched hands flattened against an unseen barrier. Slowly, he swept his hands right and left, sure that he was touching the wall of his cell. Yet his eyes told him he was on a mountain side, and every sight, sound, and smell was making it real to him.

Puzzled, he thought a moment and then, finding an explanation that satisfied him, he nodded once and went back to sit at ease on his bunk. This must be some superior form of TV that included odors, the illusion of wind, and other fancy touches to make it more vivid. The total effect was so convincing that

Ross had to keep reminding himself that it was all just a picture.

The wolf was dead. Its pack mates had fled into the brush, but since the picture remained, Ross decided that the show was not yet over. He could still hear a click of sound, and he waited for the next bit of action. But the reason for his viewing it still eluded him.

A man came into view, crossing before Ross. He stooped to examine the dead wolf, catching it by the tail and hoisting its hindquarters off the ground. Comparing the beast's size with the hunter's, Ross saw that he had not been wrong in his estimation of the animal's unusually large dimensions. The man shouted over his shoulder, his words distinct enough, but unintelligible to Ross.

The stranger was oddly dressed—too lightly dressed if one judged the climate by the frequent snow patches and the biting cold. A strip of coarse cloth, extending from his armpit to about four inches above the knee, was wound about his body and pulled in at the waist by a belt. The belt, far more ornate than the cumbersome wrapping, was made of many small chains linking metal plates and supported a long dagger which hung straight in front. The man also wore a round blue cloak, now swept back on his shoulders to free his bare arms, which was fastened by a large pin under his chin. His footgear, which extended above his calves, was made of animal hide, still bearing patches of shaggy hair. His face was beardless, though a shadowy line along his chin suggested that he had not shaved that particular day. A fur cap concealed most of his dark-brown hair.

Was he an Indian? No, for although his skin was tanned, it was as fair as Ross's under that weathering. And his clothing did not resemble any Indian apparel

Ross had ever seen. Yet, in spite of his primitive trappings, the man had such an aura of authority, of self-confidence, and competence that it was clear he was top dog in his own section of the world.

Soon another man, dressed much like the first, but with a rust-brown cloak, came along, pulling behind him two very reluctant donkeys, whose eyes rolled fearfully at sight of the dead wolf. Both animals wore packs lashed on their backs by ropes of twisted hide. Then another man came along, with another brace of donkeys. Finally, a fourth man, wearing skins for covering and with a mat of beard on his cheeks and chin, appeared. His uncovered head, a bush of uncombed flaxen hair, shone whitish as he knelt beside the dead beast, a knife with a dull-gray blade in his hand, and set to work skinning the wolf with appreciable skill. Three more pairs of donkeys, all heavily laden, were led past the scene before he finished his task. Finally, he rolled the bloody skin into a bundle and gave the flayed body a kick before he ran lightly after the disappearing train of pack animals.

2

ROSS, ABSORBED in the scene before him, was not prepared for the sudden and complete darkness which
blotted out not only the action but the light in his own
room as well.

"What—?" His startled voice rang loudly in his
ears, too loudly, for all sound had been wiped out with
the light. The faint swish of the ventilating system, of
which he had not been actively aware until it had disappeared, was also missing. A trace of the same panic
he had known in the cockpit of the atomjet tingled
along his nerves. But this time he could meet the unknown with action.

Ross slowly moved through the dark, his hands outstretched before him to ward off contact with the wall.
He was determined that somehow he would discover
the hidden door, escape from this dark cell . . .

There! His palm struck flat against a smooth surface. He swept out his hand—and suddenly it passed
over emptiness. Ross explored by touch. There *was* a
door and now it was open. For a moment he hesitated,

upset by a nagging little fear that if he stepped through he would be out on the hillside with the wolves.

"That's stupid!" Again he spoke aloud. And, just because he did feel uneasy, he moved. All the frustrations of the past hours built up in him a raging desire to do something—anything—just so long as it was what *he* wanted to do and not at another's orders.

Nevertheless, Ross continued to move slowly, for the space beyond that open door was as deep and dark a pit as the room he left. To squeeze along one wall, using an outstretched arm as a guide, was the best procedure, he decided.

A few feet farther on, his shoulder slipped from the surface and he half tumbled into another open door. But there was the wall again, and he clung to it thankfully. Another door . . . Ross paused, trying to catch some faint sound, the slightest hint that he was not alone in this blindman's maze. But without even air currents to stir it, the blackness itself took on a thick solidity which encased him as a congealing jelly.

The wall ended. Ross kept his left hand on it, flailed out with his right, and felt his nails scrape across another surface. The space separating the two surfaces was wider than any doorway. Was it a cross-corridor? He was about to make a wider arm sweep when he heard a sound. He was not alone.

Ross went back to the wall, flattening himself against it, trying to control the volume of his own breathing in order to catch the slightest whisper of the other noise. He discovered that lack of sight can confuse the ear. He could not identify those clicks, the wisp of fluttering sound that might be air displaced by the opening of another door.

Finally, he detected something moving at floor level.

Someone or something must be creeping, not walking, toward him. Ross pushed back around the corner. It never occurred to him to challenge that crawler. There was an element of danger in this strange encounter in the dark; it was not meant to be a meeting between fellow explorers.

The sound of crawling was not steady. There were long pauses, and Ross became convinced that each rest was punctuated by heavy breathing as if the crawler was finding progress a great and exhausting effort. He fought the picture that persisted in his imagination—that of a wolf snuffling along the blacked-out hall. Caution suggested a quick retreat, but Ross's urge to rebellion held him where he was, crouching, straining to see what crept toward him.

Suddenly there was a blinding flare of light, and Ross's hands went to cover his dazzled eyes. And he heard a despairing choked exclamation from near to floor level. The same steady light that normally filled hall and room was bright again. Ross found himself standing at the juncture of two corridors—momentarily, he was absurdly pleased that he had deduced that correctly—and the crawler—?

A man—at least the figure was a two-legged, two-armed body reasonably human in outline—was lying several yards away. But the body was so wrapped in bandages and the head so totally muffled, that it lacked all identity. For that reason it was the more startling.

One of the mittened hands moved slightly, raising the body from the ground so it could squirm forward an inch or so. Before Ross could move, a man came running into the corridor from the far end. Murdock recognized Major Kelgarries. He wet his lips as the major went down on his knees beside the creature on the floor.

"Hardy! Hardy!" That voice, which carried the snap of command whenever it was addressed to Ross, was now warmly human. "Hardy, man!" The major's hands were on the bandaged body, lifting it, easing the head and shoulders back against his arm. "It's all right, Hardy. You're back—safe. This is the base, Hardy." He spoke slowly, soothingly, with the steadiness one would use to comfort a frightened child.

Those mittened paws which had beat feebly into the air fell onto the bandage-wreathed chest. "Back-safe—" The voice from behind the face mask was a rusty croak.

"Back, safe," the major assured him.

"Dark—dark all around again—" protested the croak.

"Just a power failure, man. Everything's all right now. We'll get you into bed."

The mitten pawed again until it touched Kelgarries' arm; then it flexed a little as if the hand under it was trying to grip.

"Safe—?"

"You bet you are!" The major's tone carried firm reassurance. Now Kelgarries looked up at Ross as if he knew the other had been there all the time.

"Murdock, get down to the end room. Call Dr. Farrell!"

"Yes, sir!" The "sir" came so automatically that Ross had already reached the end room before he realized he had used it.

Nobody explained matters to Ross Murdock. The bandaged Hardy was claimed by the doctor and two attendants and carried away, the major walking beside the stretcher, still holding one of the mittened hands in his. Ross hesitated, sure he was not supposed to follow, but not ready either to explore farther or return to his own room. The sight of Hardy, whoever he might be, had radically changed Ross's conception of the project he had too speedily volunteered to join.

That what they did here was important, Ross had never doubted. That it was dangerous, he had early suspected. But his awareness had been an abstract concept of danger, not connected with such concrete evidence as Hardy crawling through the dark. From the first, Ross had nursed vague plans for escape; now he knew he must get out of this place lest he end up a twin for Hardy.

"Murdock?"

Having heard no warning sound from behind, Ross whirled, ready to use his fists, his only weapons. But he did not face the major, or any of the other taciturn men he knew held positions of authority. The newcomer's brown skin was startling against the neutral shade of the walls. His hair and brows were only a few shades darker; but the general sameness of color was relieved by the vivid blue of his eyes.

Expressionless, the dark stranger stood quietly, his arms hanging loosely by his sides, studying Ross, as if the younger man was some problem he had been assigned to solve. When he spoke, his voice was a monotone lacking any modulation of feeling.

"I am Ashe." He introduced himself baldly; he might have been saying "This is a table and that is a chair."

Ross's quick temper took spark from the other's indifference. "All right—so you're Ashe!" He strove to make a challenge of it. "And what is that supposed to mean?"

But the other did not rise to the bait. He shrugged. "For the time being we have been partnered—"

"Partnered for what?" demanded Ross, controlling his temper.

"We work in pairs here. The machine sorts us . . ." he answered briefly and consulted his wrist watch. "Mess call soon."

Ashe had already turned away, and Ross could not stand the other's lack of interest. While Murdock refused to ask questions of the major or any others on that side of the fence, surely he could get some information from a fellow "volunteer."

"What is this place, anyway?" he asked.

The other glanced back over his shoulder. "Operation Retrograde."

Ross swallowed his anger. "Okay, but what do they do here? Listen, I just saw a fellow who'd been banged up as if he'd been in a concrete mixer, creeping along this hall. What sort of work do they do here? And what do we have to do?"

To his amazement Ashe smiled, at least his lips quirked faintly. "Hardy got under your skin, eh? Well, we have our percentage of failures. They are as few as it's humanly possible to make, and they give us every advantage that can be worked out for us—"

"Failures at what?"

"Operation Retrograde."

Somewhere down the hall a buzzer gave a muted whirr.

"That's mess call. And I'm hungry, even if you're not." Ashe walked away as if Ross Murdock had ceased to exist.

But Ross Murdock did exist, and to him that was an important fact. As he trailed along behind Ashe he determined that he was going to continue to exist, in one piece and unharmed, Operation Retrograde or no Operation Retrograde. And he was going to pry a few enlightening answers out of somebody very soon.

To his surprise he found Ashe waiting for him at the

door of a room from which came the sound of voices and a subdued clatter of trays and tableware.

"Not many in tonight," Ashe commented in a take-it-or-leave-it tone. "It's been a busy week."

The room was rather sparsely occupied. Five tables were empty, while the men gathered at the remaining two. Ross counted ten men, either already eating or coming back from a serving hatch with well-filled trays. All of them were dressed in slacks, shirt, and moccasins like himself—the outfit seemed to be a sort of undress uniform—and six of them were ordinary in physical appearance. The other four differed so radically that Ross could barely conceal his amazement.

Since their fellows accepted them without comment, Ross silently stole glances at them as he waited behind Ashe for a tray. One pair were clearly Oriental; they were small, lean men with thin brackets of long black mustache on either side of their mobile mouths. Yet he caught a word or two of their conversation, and they spoke his own language with the facility of the native born. In addition to the mustaches, each wore a blue tattoo mark on the forehead and others of the same design on the backs of their agile hands.

The second duo were even more fantastic. The color of their flaxen hair was normal, but they wore it in braids long enough to swing across their powerful shoulders, a fashion unlike any Ross had ever seen. Yet any suggestion of effeminacy certainly did not survive beyond the first glance at their ruggedly masculine features.

"Gordon!" One of the braided giants swung halfway around from the table to halt Ashe as he came down the aisle with his tray. "When did you get back? And where is Sanford?"

One of the Orientals laid down the spoon with which he had been vigorously stirring his coffee and asked with real concern, "Another loss?"

Ashe shook his head. "Just reassignment. Sandy's holding down Outpost Gog and doing well." He grinned and his face came to life with an expression of impish humor Ross would not have believed possible. "He'll end up with a million or two if he doesn't watch out. He takes to trade as if he were born with a beaker in his fist."

The Oriental laughed and then glanced at Ross. "Your new partner, Ashe?"

Some of the animation disappeared from Ashe's brown face; he was noncommittal again. "Temporary assignment. This is Murdock." The introduction was flat enough to daunt Ross. "Hodaki, Feng," he indicated the two Easterners with a nod as he put down his tray. "Jansen, Van Wyke." That accounted for the blonds.

"Ashe!" A man arose at the other table and came to stand beside theirs. Thin, with a dark, narrow face and restless eyes, he was much younger than the others, younger and not so well controlled. He might answer questions if there was something in it for him, Ross decided, and led the thought away.

"Well, Kurt?" Ashe's recognition was as dampening as it could be, and Ross's estimation of the younger man went up a fraction when the snub appeared to have no effect upon him.

"Did you hear about Hardy?"

Feng looked as if he were about to speak, and Van Wyke frowned. Ashe made a deliberate process of chewing and swallowing before he replied. "Naturally." His tone reduced whatever had happened to Hardy to a matter-of-fact proceeding far removed from Kurt's implied melodrama.

"He's smashed up . . . kaput . . ." Kurt's accent, slight in the beginning, was thickening. "Tortured . . ."

Ashe regarded him levelly. "You aren't on Hardy's run, are you?"

Still Kurt refused to be quashed. "Of course, I'm not! You know the run I am in training for. But that is not saying that such can not happen as well on my run, or yours, or yours!" He pointed a stabbing finger at Feng and then at the blond men.

"You can fall out of bed and break your neck, too, if your number comes up that way," observed Jansen. "Go cry on Millaird's shoulder if it hurts you that much. You were told the score at your briefing. You know why you were picked, what might happen . . ."

Ross caught a faint glance aimed at him by Ashe. He was still totally in the dark, but he would not try to pry any information from this crowd. Maybe part of their training was this hush-hush business. He would wait and see, until he could get Kurt aside and do a little pumping. Meanwhile he ate stolidly and tried to cover up his interest in the conversation.

"Then you are going to keep on saying 'Yes, sir,' 'No, sir,' to every order here—?"

Hodaki slammed his tattooed hand on the table. "Why this foolishness, Kurt? You well know how and why we are picked for runs. Hardy had the deck stacked against him through no fault of the project. That has happened before; it will happen again—"

"Which is what I have been saying! Do you wish it to happen to you? Pretty games those tribesmen on your run play with their prisoners, do they not?"

"Oh, shut up!" Jansen got to his feet. Since he loomed at least five inches above Kurt and probably could have broken him in two over one massive knee, his order was one to be considered. "If you have any complaints, go make them to Millaird. And, little man"—he poked a massive forefinger into Kurt's chest—"wait until you make that first run of yours before you sound off so loudly. No one is sent out without every advance, and Hardy was unlucky. That's that. We got him back, and that was lucky for him. He'd be the first to tell you so." He stretched. "I'm for a game—Ashe? Hodaki?"

"Always so energetic," murmured Ashe, but he nodded as did the small Oriental.

Feng smiled at Ross. "Always these three try to beat each other, and so far all the contests are draws. But we hope . . . yes, we have hopes . . ."

So Ross had no chance to speak to Kurt. Instead, he was drawn into the knot of men who, having finished their meal, entered a small arena with a half circle of spectator seats at one side and a space for contestants at the other. What followed absorbed Ross as completely as the earlier scene of the wolf killing. This too was a fight, but not a physical struggle. All three contenders were not only unlike in body, but as Ross speedily came to understand, they were also unlike in their mental approach to any problem.

They seated themselves crosslegged at the three points of a triangle. Then Ashe looked from the tall blond to the small Oriental. "Territory?" he asked crisply.

"Inland plains!" That came almost in chorus, and each man, looking at his opponent, began to laugh.

Ashe himself chuckled. "Trying to be smart tonight, boys?" he inquired. "All right, plains it is."

He brought his hand down on the floor before him, and to Ross's astonishment the area around the players darkened and the floor became a stretch of miniature countryside. Grassy plains rippled under the wind of a fair day.

"Red!"

"Blue!"

"Yellow!"

The choices came quickly from the dusk masking the players. And upon those orders points of the designated color came into being as small lights.

"Red—caravan!" Ross recognized Jansen's boom.

"Blue—raiders!" Hodaki's choice was only an instant behind.

"Yellow—unknown factor."

Ross was sure that sigh came from Jansen. "Is the unknown factor a natural phenomenon?"

"No—tribe on the march."

"Ah!" Hodaki was considering that. Ross could picture his shrug.

The game began. Ross had heard of chess, of war games played with miniature armies or ships, of games on paper which demand from the players a quick wit and a trained memory. This game, however, was all those combined, and more. As his imagination came to life, the moving points of light were transformed into the raiders, the merchants' caravan, the tribe on the march. There was ingenious deployment, a battle, a retreat, a small victory here, to be followed by a bigger defeat there. The game might have gone on for hours. The men about him muttered, taking sides and arguing heatedly in voices low enough not to drown out the moves called by the players. Ross was thrilled when the red traders avoided a very cleverly laid ambush, and indignant when the tribe was forced to withdraw or the caravan lost points. It was the most fascinating game he had ever seen, and he realized that the three men ordering these moves were all masters of strategy. Their respective skills checkmated each other so equally that an outright win was far away.

Then Jansen laughed, and the red line of the caravan gathered in a tight knot. "Camped at a spring," he announced, "but with plenty of sentries out." Red sparks showed briefly beyond that center core. "And they'll have to stay there for all of me. We could keep this up till doomsday, and nobody would crack."

"No"—Hodaki contradicted him—"someday one of you will make a little mistake and then—"

"And then whatever bully boys you're running will clobber us?" asked Jansen. "That'll be the day! Anyway, truce for now."

"Granted!"

The lights of the arena went on and the plains vanished into a dark, tiled floor. "Any time you want a return engagement it'll be fine with me," said Ashe, getting up.

Jansen grinned. "Put that off for a month or so, Gordon. We push into time tomorrow. Take care of yourselves, you two. I don't want to have to break in another set of players when I come back."

Ross, finding it difficult to shake off the illusion which had held him entranced, felt a slight touch on his shoulder and glanced up. Kurt stood behind him, apparently intent upon Jansen and Hodaki as they argued over some point of the game.

"See you tonight." The boy's lips hardly moved, a trick Ross knew from his own past. Yes, he *would* see Kurt tonight, or whenever he could. He was going to learn what it was this odd company seemed determined to keep as their own private secret.

3

Ross STOOD cautiously against the wall of his darkened room, his head turned toward the slightly open door. A slight shuffling sound had awakened him, and he was now as ready as a cat before her spring. But he did not hurl himself at the figure now easing the door farther open. He waited until the visitor was approaching the bunk before he slid along the wall, closing the door and putting his shoulders against it.

"What's the pitch?" Ross demanded in a whisper.

There was a ragged breath, maybe two, then a little laugh out of the dark. "You are ready?" The visitor's accent left no doubt as to his identity. Kurt was paying him the promised visit.

"Did you think that I wouldn't be?"

"No." The dim figure sat without invitation on the edge of the bunk. "I would not be here otherwise, Murdock. You are plenty . . . have plenty on the ball. You see, I have heard things about you. Like me, you were tricked into this game. Tell me, is it not true that you saw Hardy tonight."

"You hear a lot, don't you?" Ross was noncommittal.

"I hear, I see, I learn more than these big mouths, like the major with his do's and don'ts. That I can tell you! You saw Hardy. Do *you* want to be a Hardy?"

"Is there any danger of that?"

"Danger!" Kurt snorted. "Danger—you have not yet known the meaning of danger, little man. Not until now. I ask you again, do you want to end like Hardy? They have not yet looped you in with all their big talk. That is why I came here tonight. If you know what is good for you, Murdock, you will make a break before they tape you—"

"Tape me?"

Kurt's laugh was full of anger, not amusement. "Oh, yes. They have many tricks here. They are big brains, eggheads, all of them with their favorite gadgets. They put you through a machine to get you registered on tape. Then, my boy, you cannot get outside the base without ringing all the alarms! Neat, eh? So if you want to make a break, you must try it before they tape you."

Ross did not trust Kurt, but he was listening to him attentively. The other's argument sounded convincing to one whose general ignorance of science led him to believe that all kinds of weird inventions were entirely possible and probable—usually to be produced in some dim future, but perhaps today.

"They must have you taped," Ross pointed out.

Kurt laughed again, but this time he was amused. "They believe that they have. Only they are not as smart as they believe, the major and the rest, including Millaird! No, I have a fighting chance to get out of this place, only I cannot do it alone. That is why I have been waiting for them to bring in a new guy I could get to before they had him pinned down for good. You are tough, Murdock. I saw your record, and I'm betting that you did not come here with the intention of staying. So—here is your chance to go along with one who knows the ropes. You will not have such a good one again."

The longer Kurt talked, the more convincing he was. Ross lost a few of his suspicions. It was true that he had come prepared to run at the first possible opportunity, and if Kurt had everything planned, so much the better. Of course, it was possible that Kurt was a stool pigeon, leading him on as a test. But that was a chance Ross would have to take.

"Look here, Murdock, maybe you think it's easy to break out of here. Do you know where we are, boy? We're near enough to the North Pole as makes no difference! Are you going to leg it back some hundreds of miles through thick ice and snow? A nice jaunt if you make it. I do not think that you can—not without plans and a partner who knows what he is about."

"And how *do* we go? Steal one of those atomjets? I'm no pilot—are you?"

"They have other things besides a-j's here. This place is strictly hush-hush. Even the a-j's do not set down too often for fear they will be tracked by radar. Where have you been, boy? Don't you know the Reds are circling around up here? These fellows watch for Red activity, and the Reds watch them. They play it under the table on both sides. We get our supplies overland by cats—"

"Cats?"

"Snow sleds, like tractors," the other answered impatiently. "Our stuff is dumped miles to the south, and the cats go down once a month to bring it back.

There's no trick to driving a cat, and they tear off the miles—"

"How many miles to the south?" inquired Ross skeptically. Granted Kurt was speaking the truth, travel over an arctic wilderness in a stolen machine was risky, to say the least. Ross had only a very vague idea of the polar regions, but he was sure that they could easily swallow up the unwary forever.

"Maybe only a hundred or so, boy. But I have more than one plan, and I'm willing to risk *my* neck. Do you think I intend to start out blind?"

There was that, of course. Ross had early sized up his visitor as one who was first of all interested in his own welfare. He wouldn't risk his neck without a definite plan in mind.

"Well, what do you say, Murdock? Are you with me or not?"

"I'll take some time to chew it over—"

"Time is what you do not have, boy. Tomorrow they will tape you. Then—no over the wall for you."

"Suppose you tell me your trick for fooling the tape," Ross countered.

"That I cannot do, seeing as how it lies in the way my brain is put together. Do you think I can break open my skull and hand you a piece of what is inside? No, you jump with me tonight or else I must wait to grab the next one who lands here."

Kurt stood up. His last words were spoken matter-of-factly, and Ross believed he meant exactly what he said. But Ross hesitated. He wanted to try for freedom, a desire fed by his suspicions of what was going on here. He neither liked nor trusted Kurt, but he thought he understood him—better than he understood Ashe or the others. Also, with Kurt he was sure he could hold his own; it would be the kind of struggle he had experienced before.

"Tonight . . ." he repeated slowly.

"Yes, tonight!" There was new eagerness in Kurt's voice, for he sensed that the other was wavering. "I have been preparing for a long time, but there must be two of us. We have to take turns driving the cat. There can be no rest until we are far to the south. I tell you it will be easy. There are food caches arranged along the route for emergencies. I have a map marked to show where they are. Are you coming?"

When Ross did not answer at once the other moved closer to him.

"Remember Hardy? He was not the first, and he will not be the last. They use us up fast here. That is why they brought you so quickly. I tell you, it is better to take your chance with me than on a run."

"And what is a run?"

"So they have not briefed you? Well, a run is a little jaunt back into history—not nice comfortable history such as you learned out of a book when you were a little kid. No, you are dropped back into some savage time before history—"

"That's impossible!"

"Yes? You saw those two big blond boys tonight, did you not? Why do you suppose they sport those braids? Because they are taking a little trip into the time when he-men wore braids, and carried axes big enough to crack a man open! And Hodaki and his partner . . . Ever hear of the Tartars? Maybe you have not, but once they nearly overran most of Europe."

Ross swallowed. He now knew where he had seen braids pictured on warriors—the Vikings! And Tartars, yes, that movie about someone named Khan, Genghis Kahn! But to return into the past was impossible.

Yet, he remembered the picture he had watched to-day with the wolf slayer and the shaggy-haired man who wore skins. Neither of these was of his own world! Could Kurt be telling the truth? Ross's vivid memory of the scene he had witnessed made Kurt's story more convincing.

"Suppose you get sent back to a time where they do not like strangers," Kurt continued. "Then you are in for it. That is what happened to Hardy. And it is not good—not good at all!"

"But why?"

Kurt snorted. "*That* they do not tell you until just before you take your first run. I do not want to know why. But I do know that I am not going to be sent into any wilderness where a savage may run a spear through me just to prove something or other for Major John Kelgarries, or for Millaird either. I will try my plan first."

The urgency in Kurt's protest carried Ross past the wavering point. He, too, would try the cat. He was only familiar with this time and world; he had no desire to be sent into another one.

Once Ross had made his decision, Kurt hurried him into action. Kurt's knowledge of the secret procedures at the base proved excellent. Twice they were halted by locked doors, but only momentarily, for Kurt had a tiny gadget, concealed in the palm of his hand, which had only to be held over a latch to open a recalcitrant door.

There was enough light in the corridors to give them easy passage, but the rooms were dark, and twice Kurt had to lead Ross by the hand, avoiding furniture or installations with the surety of one who had practiced that same route often. Murdock's opinion of his companion's ability underwent several upward revisions during that tour, and he began to believe that he was really in luck to have found such a partner.

In the last room, Ross willingly followed Kurt's orders to put on the fur clothing Kurt passed to him. The fit was not exact, but he surmised that Kurt had chosen as well as possible. A final door opened, and they stepped out into the polar night of winter. Kurt's mittened hand grasped Ross's, pulling him along. Together, they pushed back the door of a hangar shed to get at their escape vehicle.

The cat was a strange machine, but Ross was given no time to study it. He was shoved into the cockpit, a bubble covering settled down over them, closing them in, and the engine came to life under Kurt's urging. The cat must be traveling at its best pace, Ross thought. Yet the crawl which took them away from the mounded snow covering the base seemed hardly better than a man could make afoot.

For a short time Kurt headed straight away from the starting point, but Ross soon heard him counting slowly to himself as if he were timing something. At the count of twenty the cat swung to the right and made a wide half circle which was copied at the next count of twenty by a similar sweep in the opposite direction. After his pattern had been repeated for six turns, Ross found it difficult to guess whether they had ever returned to their first course. When Kurt stopped counting he asked, "Why the dance pattern?"

"Would you rather be scattered in little pieces all over the landscape?" the other snapped. "The base doesn't need fences two miles high to keep us in, or others out; they take other precautions. You should thank fortune we got through that first mine field without blowing . . ."

Ross swallowed, but he refused to let Kurt know that he was rattled. "So it isn't as easy to get away as you said?"

"Shut up!" Kurt began counting again, and Ross had some cold apprehensive moments in which to reflect upon the folly of quick decisions and wonder bleakly why he had not thought things through before he leaped.

Again they sketched a weaving pattern in the snow, but this time the arcs formed acute angles. Ross glanced now and then at the intent man at the wheel. How had Kurt managed to memorize this route? His urge to escape the base must certainly be a strong one.

Back and forth they crawled, gaining only a few yards in each of those angled strikes to right or left.

"Good thing cats are atomic powered," Kurt commented during one of the intervals between mine fields. "We'd run out of fuel otherwise."

Ross fought down the impulse to move his feet away from any possible contact point with the engine. These machines must be safe to ride in, but the bogy of radiation was frightening. Luckily, Kurt was now back to a straight track, with no more weaving.

"We are out!" Kurt said with exultation. But he added no more than just the reassurance of their escape.

The cat crawled on. To Ross's eyes there was no trail to follow, no guideposts, yet Kurt steered ahead with confidence. A little later he pulled to a stop and said to Ross, "We have to drive turn and turn about —your turn."

Ross was dubious. "Well, I can drive a car—but this—"

"Is fool proof." Kurt caught him up. "The worst was getting through the mine fields, and we are out of that now. See here—" his hand made a shadow on the lighted instrument panel, "this will keep you straight. If you can steer a car, you can steer this. Watch!" He started up again and once more he swung the cat to the left.

A light on the panel began to blink at a rate which increased rapidly as they veered farther away from their original course.

"See? You keep that light steady, and you are on course. If it begins to blink, you cast about until it steadies again. Simple enough for a baby. Take over and see."

It was hard to change places in the sealed cabin of the cat, but they were successful, and Ross took the wheel gingerly. Following Kurt's directions, he started ahead, his eyes focused on the light rather than the white expanse before him. And after a few minutes of strain he caught the hang of it. As Kurt had promised, it was very simple. After watching him for a while, his instructor gave a grunt of satisfaction and settled down for a nap.

Once the first excitement of driving the cat wore off, the operation tended to become monotonous. Ross caught himself yawning, but he kept at his post with dogged stubbornness. This had been Kurt's game all the way through—so far—and he was certainly not going to resign his first chance to show that he could be of use also. If there had only been some break in the eternal snow, some passing light or goal to be seen ahead, it would not have been so bad. Finally, every now and then, Ross had to jiggle off course just enough so that the warning blink of light would alert him and keep him from falling asleep. He was unaware that Kurt had awakened during one of those maneuvers until the other spoke. "Your own private alarm clock, Murdock? Okay, I do not quarrel with anyone who uses his head. But you had better get some shut-eye, or we will not keep rolling."

Ross was too tired to protest. They changed places, and he curled up as best he could on his small share of the seat. Only now that he was free to sleep, he realized he no longer wanted to. Kurt must have thought Ross had fallen asleep, for after perhaps two miles of steady grinding along, he moved cautiously behind the wheel. Ross saw by the trace of light from the instrument panel that his companion was digging into the breast of his parka to bring out a small object which he held against the wheel of the cat with one hand, while with the other he tapped out an irregular rhythm.

To Ross the action made no sense. But he did not miss the other's sigh of relief as he restored his treasure to hiding once more, as if some difficult task was now behind him. Shortly afterward the cat ground to a stop, and Ross sat up, rubbing his eyes. "What's the matter? Engine trouble?"

Kurt had folded his arms across the wheel. "No. It just that we are to wait here—"

"Wait? For what? Kelgarries to come along and pick us up?"

Kurt laughed. "The major? How I wish that he *would* arrive presently. What a surprise he would receive! Not two little mice to be put back into their cages, but the tiger cat, all claws and fangs!"

Ross sat up straighter. This now had the bad smell of a frame, a frame with himself planted right in the middle. He figured out the possibilities and came up with an answer which would smear Ross Murdock all over any map. If Kurt were waiting to meet friends out here, they could only be of one brand.

For most of his short life Ross had been engaged in

a private war against the restrictions imposed upon him by a set of legal rules to which something within him would not conform. And he had, during those same years filled with attacks, retreats, and strategic maneuvering, formulated a code of rules by which to play his dangerous game. He had not murdered, and he would never follow the path Kurt took. To one who was supremely impatient of restraint, the methods and aims of Kurt's employers were not only impossibly fantastic and illogical—they were to be opposed to the last ounce of any man's energy.

"Your friends late?" He tried to sound casual.

"Not yet, and if you now plan to play the hero, Murdock, think better of it!" Kurt's tone held the crack of an order—that note Ross had so much disliked in the major's voice. "This is an operation which has been most carefully planned and upon which a great deal depends. No one shall spoil it for us now—"

"The Reds planted you on the project, eh?" Ross wanted to keep the other talking to give himself a chance to think. And this was one time he had to think, clearly and with speed.

"There is no need for me to tell you the sad tale of my life, Murdock. And you would doubtless find much of it boring. If you wish to continue to live—for a while, at least—you will remain quiet and do as you are told."

Kurt must be armed, for he would not be so confident unless he had a weapon he could now turn on Ross. On the other hand, if what Ross guessed were true, this *was* the time to play the hero—when there was only Kurt to handle. Better to be a dead hero than a live captive in the hands of Kurt's dear friends across the pole.

Without warning, Ross threw his body to the left, striving to pin Kurt against the driver's side of the cabin, his hands clawing at the fur ruff bordering the other's hood, trying for a throat hold. Perhaps it was Kurt's over-confidence which betrayed him and left him open to a surprise attack. He struggled hard to bring up his arm, but both his weight and Ross's held him tight. Ross caught at his wrist, noticing a gleam of metal.

They threshed about, the bulkiness of the fur clothing hampering them. Ross wondered fleetingly why the other had not made sure of him earlier. As it was he fought with all his vigor to keep Kurt immobile, to try and knock him out with a lucky blow.

In the end Kurt aided in his own defeat. When Ross relaxed somewhat, the other pushed against him, only to have Ross flinch to one side. Kurt could not stop himself, and his head cracked against the wheel of the cat. He went limp.

Ross made the most of the next few moments. He brought his belt from under his parka, twisting it around Kurt's wrists with no gentleness. Then he wriggled about, changing places with the unconscious man.

He had no idea of where to go, but he was sure he was going to get away—at the cat's top speed—from that point. And with that in mind and only a limited knowledge of how to manage the machine, Ross started up and turned in a wide circle until he was sure the cat was headed in the opposite direction.

The light which had guided them was still on. Would reversing its process take him back to the base? Lost in the immensity of the cold wilderness, he made the only choice possible and gunned the cat again.

4

ONCE AGAIN Ross sat waiting for others to decide his future. He was as outwardly composed as he had been in Judge Rawle's chambers, but inwardly he was far more apprehensive. Out in the wilderness of the polar night he had had no chance for escape. Heading away from Kurt's rendezvous, Ross had run straight into the search party from the base, had seen in action that mechanical hound that Kurt had said they would put on the fugitive's trail—the thing which would have gone on hunting them until its metal rusted into powder. Kurt's boasted immunity to that tracker had not been as good as he had believed, though it had won them a start.

Ross did not know just how much it might count in his favor that he had been on his way back, with Kurt a prisoner in the cat. As his waiting hours wore on he began to think it might mean very little indeed. This time there was no show on the wall of his cell, nothing but time to think—too much of that—and no pleasant things to think about.

But he had learned one valuable lesson on that cold expedition. Kelgarries and the others at the base were the most formidable opponents he had ever met, and all the balance of luck and equipment lay on their side of the scales. Ross was now convinced that there could be no escape from this base. He had been impressed by Kurt's preparations, knowing that some of them were far beyond anything he himself could have devised. He did not doubt that Kurt had come here fully prepared with every ingenious device the Reds could supply.

At least Kurt's friends had had a rude welcome when they did arrive at the meeting place. Kelgarries had heard Ross out and then had sent ahead a team. Before Ross's party had reached the base there had been a blast which split the arctic night wide open. And Kurt, conscious by then, had shown his only sign of emotion when he realized what it meant.

The door to Ross's cell room clicked, and he swung his feet to the floor, sitting up on his bunk to face his future. This time he made no attempt to put on an act. He was not in the least sorry he had tried to get away. Had Kurt been on the level, it would have been a bright play. That Kurt was not, was just plain bad luck.

Kelgarries and Ashe entered, and at the sight of Ashe the taut feeling in Ross's middle loosened a bit. The major might come by himself to pass sentence, but he would not bring Ashe along if the sentence was a really harsh one.

"You got off to a bad start here, Murdock." The major sat down on the edge of the wall shelf which doubled as a table. "You're going to have a second chance, so consider yourself lucky. We know you aren't another plant of our enemies, a fact that saves your neck. Do you have anything to add to your story?"

"No, sir." He was not adding that "sir" to curry any favor; it came naturally when one answered Kelgarries.

"But you have some questions?"

Ross met that with the truth. "A lot of them."

"Why don't you ask them?"

Ross smiled thinly, an expression far removed and years older than his bashful boy's grin of the shy act. "A wise guy doesn't spill his ignorance. He uses his eyes and ears and keeps his trap shut—"

"And goes off half cocked as a result . . ." the major added. "I don't think you would have enjoyed the company of Kurt's paymaster."

"I didn't know about him then—not when I left here."

"Yes, and when you discovered the truth, you took steps. Why?" For the first time there was a trace of feeling in the major's voice.

"Because I don't like the line-up on his side of the fence."

"That single fact has saved your neck this time, Murdock. Step out of line once more, and nothing will help you. But just so we won't have to worry about that, suppose you ask a few of those questions."

"How much of what Kurt fed me is the truth?" Ross blurted out. "I mean all that stuff about shooting back in time."

"All of it." The major said it so quietly that it carried complete conviction.

"But why—how—?"

"You have us on a spot, Murdock. Because of your little expedition, we have to tell you more now than we tell any of our men before the final briefing. Listen, and forget all of it except what applies to the job at hand.

"The Reds shot up Sputnik and then Muttnik. When—? Twenty-five years ago. We got up our answers a little later. There were a couple of spectacular crashes on the moon, then that space station that didn't stay in orbit, after that—stalemate. In the past quarter century we've had no voyages into space, nothing that was prophesied. Too many bugs, too many costly failures. Finally we began to get hints of something big, bigger than any football roaming the heavens.

"Any discovery in science comes about by steps. It can be traced back through those steps by another scientist. But suppose you were confronted by a result which apparently had been produced without any preliminaries. What would be your guess concerning it?"

Ross stared at the major. Although he didn't see what all this had to do with time-jumping, he sensed that Kelgarries was waiting for a serious answer, that somehow Ross would be judged by his reply.

"Either that the steps were kept strictly secret," he said slowly, "or that the result didn't rightfully belong to the man who said he discovered it."

For the first time the major regarded him with approval. "Suppose this discovery was vital to your life —what would you do?"

"Try to find the source!"

"There you have it! Within the past five years our friends across the way have come up with three such discoveries. One we were able to trace, duplicate, and use, with a few refinements of our own. The other two remain rootless; yet they are linked with the first. We are now attempting to solve that problem, and the time grows late. For some reason, though the Reds now have their super, super gadgets, they are not yet ready to use them. Sometimes the things work, and sometimes they fail. Everything points to the fact that the Reds are now experimenting with discoveries which are not basically their own—"

"Where did they get them? From another world?" Ross's imagination came to life. Had a successful space voyage been kept secret? Had there been contact made with another intelligent race?

"In a way it's another world, but the world of time —not space. Seven years ago we got a man out of East Berlin. He was almost dead, but he lived long enough to record on tape some amazing data, so wild it was almost dismissed as the ravings of delirium. But that was after Sputnik, and we didn't dare disregard any hints from the other side of the Iron Curtain. So the recording was turned over to our scientists, who proved it had a core of truth.

"Time travel has been written up in fiction; it has been discussed otherwise as an impossibility. Then we discover that the Reds have it working—"

"You mean, they go into the future and bring back machines to use now."

The major shook his head. "Not the future, the past."

Was this an elaborate joke? Somewhat heatedly Ross snapped out the answer to that. "Look here, I know I haven't the education of your big brains, but I do know that the farther back you go into history the simpler things are. We ride in cars; only a hundred years ago men drove horses. We have guns; go back a little and you'll find them waving swords and shooting guys with bows and arrows—those that don't wear tin plate on them to stop being punctured—"

"Only they were, after all," commented Ashe. "Look at Agincourt, m'lad, and remember what arrows did to the French knights in armor."

Ross disregarded the interruption. "Anyway" he stuck doggedly to his point—"the farther back you go, the simpler things are. How are the Reds going to find anything in history we can't beat today?"

"That is a point which has baffled us for several years now," the major returned. "Only it is not *how* they are going to find it, but *where*. Because somewhere in the past of this world they have contacted a civilization able to produce weapons and ideas so advanced as to baffle our experts. We have to find that source and either mine it ourselves or close it off. As yet we're still trying to find it."

Ross shook his head. "It must be a long way back. Those guys who discover tombs and dig up old cities —couldn't they give you some hints? Wouldn't a civilization like that have left something we could find today?"

"It depends," Ashe remarked, "upon the type of civilization. The Egyptians built in stone, grandly. They used tools and weapons of copper, bronze, and stone, and they were considerate enough to operate in a dry climate which preserved relics well. The cities of the Fertile Crescent built in mudbrick and used stone, copper, and bronze tools. They also chose a portion of the world where climate was a factor in keeping their memory green.

"The Greeks built in stone, wrote their books, kept their history to bequeath it to their successors, and so did the Romans. And on this side of the ocean the Incas, the Mayas, the unknown races before them, and the Aztecs of Mexico all built in stone and worked in metal. And stone and metal survive. But what if there had been an early people who used plastics and brittle alloys, who had no desire to build permanent buildings, whose tools and artifacts were meant to wear out quickly, perhaps for economic reasons? What would they leave us—considering, perhaps, that an ice age had intervened between their time and ours, with glaciers to grind into dust what little they did possess?

"There is evidence that the poles of our world have changed and that this northern region was once close to being tropical. Any catastrophe violent enough to bring about a switch in the poles of this planet might well have wiped out all traces of a civilization, no matter how superior. We have good reason to believe that such a people must have existed, but we must find them."

"And Ashe is a convert from the skeptics—" the major slipped down from his perch on the wall shelf —"he is an archaeologist, one of your tomb discoverers, and knows what he is talking about. We must do our hunting in time earlier than the first pyramid, earlier than the first group of farmers who settled by the Tigris River. But we have to let the enemy guide us to it. That's where you come in."

"Why me?"

"That is a question to which our psychologists are still trying to find the answer, my young friend. It seems that the majority of the people of several nations linked together in this project have become too civilized. The reactions of most men to given sets of circumstances have become set in regular patterns and they cannot break that conditioning, or if personal danger forces them to change those patterns, they are afterward so adrift they cannot function at their highest potential. Teach a man to kill, as in war, and then you have to recondition him later.

"But during these same wars we also develop another type. He is the born commando, the secret agent, the expendable man who lives on action. There are not many of this kind, and they are potent weapons. In peacetime that particular collection of emotions, nerve, and skills becomes a menace to the very society he has fought to preserve during a war. He is pressured by the peaceful environment into becoming a criminal or a misfit.

"The men we send out from here to explore the past are not only given the best training we can possibly supply for them, but they are all of the type once heralded as the frontiersman. History is sentimental about that type—when he is safely dead—but the present finds him difficult to live with. Our time agents are misfits in the modern world because their inherited abilities are born out of season now. They must be young enough and possess a certain brand of intelligence to take the stiff training and to adapt, and they must pass our tests. Do you understand?"

Ross nodded. "You want crooks because they are crooks?"

"No, not because they are crooks, but because they are misfits in their time and place. Don't, I beg of you, Murdock, think that we are operating a penal institution here. You would never have been recruited if you hadn't tested out to suit us. But the man who may be labeled murderer in his own period might rank as a hero in another, an extreme example, but true. When we train a man he not only can survive in the period to which he is sent, but he can also pass as a native born in that era—"

"What about Hardy?"

The major gazed into space. "There is no operation which is foolproof. We have never said that we don't run into trouble or that there is no danger in this. We have to deal with both natives of different times, and if we are lucky and hit a hot run, with the Reds. They suspect that we are casting about, hunting their trail. They managed to plant Kurt Vogel on us. He had an almost perfect cover and conditioning. Now you have it straight, Murdock. You satisfy our tests, and you'll be given a chance to say yes or no before your first run. If you say no and refuse duty, it means you must become an exile and stay here. No man who has gone through our training can return to normal life; there is too much chance of his being picked up and sweated by the opposition."

"Never?"

The major shrugged. "This may be a long-term operation. We hope not, but there is no way of telling now. You will be in exile until we either find what we want or fail entirely. That is the last card I have to lay on the table." He stretched. "You're slated for training tomorrow. Think it over and then let us know your answer when the time comes. Meanwhile, you are to be teamed with Ashe, who will see to putting you through the course."

It was a big hunk to swallow, but once down, Ross found it digestible. The training opened up a whole new world to him. Judo and wrestling were easy enough to absorb, and he thoroughly enjoyed the workouts. But the patient hours of archery practice, the strict instruction in the use of a long-bladed bronze dagger were more demanding. The mastering of one new language and then another, the intensive drill in unfamiliar social customs, the memorizing of strict taboos and ethics were difficult. Ross learned to keep records in knots on hide thongs and was inducted into the art of primitive bargaining and trade. He came to understand the worth of a cross-shaped tin ingot compared to a string of amber beads and some well-cured white furs. He now understood why he had been shown a traders' caravan during that first encounter with the purpose behind Operation Retrograde.

During the training days his feeling toward Ashe changed materially. A man could not work so closely with another and continue to resent his attitude; either he blew up entirely, or he learned to adjust. His awe at Ashe's vast amount of practical knowledge, freely offered to serve his own blundering ignorance, created a respect for the man which might have become friendship, had Ashe ever relaxed his own shield of impersonal efficiency. Ross did not try to breach the barrier between them mainly because he was sure that the reason for it was the fact that he was a "volunteer." It gave him an odd new feeling he avoided trying to analyze. He had always had a kind of pride in his record; now he had begun to wish sometimes that it was a record of a different type.

Men came and went. Hodaki and his partner disappeared, as did Jansen and his. One lost track of time within that underground warren which was the base. Ross gradually discovered that the whole establishment covered a large area under an external crust of ice and snow. There were laboratories, a well-appointed hospital, armories which stocked weapons usually seen only in museums, but which here were free of any signs of age, and ready for use. There were libraries with mile upon mile of tape recordings as well as films. Ross could not understand everything he heard and saw, but he soaked up all he could so that once or twice, when drifting off to sleep at night, he thought of himself as a sponge which had nearly reached its total limit of absorption.

He learned to wear naturally the clumsy kilt-tunic he had seen on the wolf slayer, to shave with practiced assurance, using a leaf-shaped bronze razor, to eat strange food until he relished the taste. Making lesson time serve a double duty, he lay under sunlamps while listening to tape recordings, until his skin darkened to a weathered hue resembling Ashe's. There was always talk to listen to, important talk which he was afraid to miss.

"Bronze." Ashe weighed a dagger in his hand one day. Its hilt, made of dark horn studded with an intricate pattern of tiny golden nail heads, had a gleam not unlike that of the blade. "Do you know, Murdock, that bronze can be tougher than steel? If it wasn't that iron is so much more plentiful and easier to work, we might never have come out of the Bronze Age? Iron is cheaper and easier found, and when the first smith learned to work it, an end came to one way of life, a beginning to another.

"Yes, bronze is important to us here, and so are the men who worked it. Smiths were sacred in the old days. We know that they made a secret of their trade which overrode the bounds of district, tribe, and race. A smith was welcome in any village, his person safe on the road. In fact, the roads themselves were under the protection of the gods; there was peace on them for all wayfarers. The land was wide then, and it was empty. The tribes were few and small, and there was plenty of room for the hunter, the farmer, the trader. Life was not such a scramble of man against man, but rather of man against nature—"

"No wars?" asked Ross. "Then why the bow-and-dagger drill?"

"Wars were small affairs, disputes between family clans or tribes. As for the bow, there were formidable things in the forests—giant animals, wolves, wild boars—"

"Cave bears?"

Ashe sighed with weary patience. "Get it through your head, Murdock, that history is much longer than you seem to think. Cave bears and the use of bronze weapons do not overlap. No, you will have to go back maybe several thousand years earlier and then hunt your bear with a flint-tipped spear in your hand if you are fool enough to try it."

"Or take a rifle with you." Ross made a suggestion he had longed to voice for some time.

Ashe rounded on him swiftly, and Ross knew him well enough to realize that he was seriously displeased.

"That is just what you don't do, Murdock, not from this base, as you well know by now. You take no weapon from here which is not designed for the period in which your run lies. Just as you do not become embroiled while on that run in any action which might influence the course of history."

Ross went on polishing the blade he held. "What would happen if somebody did break that rule?"

Ashe put down the dagger he had been playing with. "We don't know—we just don't know. So far we have operated in the fringe territory, keeping away from any district with a history which we can trace accurately. Maybe some day—" his eyes were on a wall of weapon racks he plainly did not see—"maybe some day we can stand and watch the rise of the pyramids, witness the march of Alexander's armies . . . But not yet. We stay away from history, and we are sure that the Reds are doing the same. It has become the old problem once presented by the atom bomb.

Nobody wants to upset the balance and take the consequences. Let us find their outpost and we'll withdraw our men from all the other runs at once."

"What makes everyone so sure that they have an outpost somewhere? Couldn't they be working right at the main source, sir?"

"They could, but for some reason they are not. As for how we know that much, it's information received." Ashe smiled thinly. "No, the source is much farther back in time than their halfway post. But if we find that, then we can trail them. So we plant men in suitable eras and hope for the best. That's a good weapon you have there, Murdock. Are you willing to wear it in earnest?"

The inflection in that question caught Ross's full attention. His gray eyes met those blue ones. This was it—at long last.

"Right away?"

Ashe picked up a belt of bronze plates strung together with chains, a twin to that Ross had seen worn by the wolf slayer. He held it out to the younger man. "You take your trial run any time—tomorrow."

Ross drew a deeper breath. "Where—to when?"

"An island which will later be Britain. When? About two thousand B.C. Beaker traders were beginning to open their stations there. This is your graduation exercise, Murdock."

Ross fitted the blade he had been polishing into the wooden sheath on the belt. "If you say I can do it, I'm willing to try."

He caught that glance Ashe shot at him, but he could not read its meaning. Annoyance? Impatience? He was still puzzling over it when the other turned abruptly and left him alone.

5

HE MIGHT have said yes, but that didn't mean, Ross discovered, that he was to be shipped off at once to early Britain. Ashe's "tomorrow" proved to be several days later. The cover was that of a Beaker trader, and Ross's impersonation was checked again and again by experts, making sure that the last detail was correct and that no suspicion of a tribesman, no mistake on Ross's part would betray him.

The Beaker people were an excellent choice for infiltration. They were not a closely knit clan; suspicious of strangers and alert to any deviation from the norm, as more race-conscious tribes might be. For they lived by trade, leaving to Ross's own time the mark of their far-flung "empire" in the beakers found in graves scattered in clusters of a handful or so from the Rhineland to Spain, and from the Balkans to Britain.

They did not depend only upon the taboo of the trade road for their safety, for the Beakermen were master bowmen. A roving people, they pushed into new territory to establish posts, living amicably among peoples with far different customs—the Downs farmers, horse herders, shore-side fisherfolk.

With Ashe, Ross passed a last inspection. Their hair had not grown long enough to require braiding, but they did have enough to hold it back from their faces with hide headbands. The kilt-tunics of coarse material, duplicating samples brought from the past, were harsh to the skin and poorly fitting. But the workmanship of their link-and-plate bronze belts, the sleek bow guards strapped to their wrists, and the bows themselves approached fine art. Ashe's round cloak was the blue of a master trader, and he wore wealth in a necklace of polished wolf's teeth alternating with amber beads. Ross's more modest position in the tribe was indicated not only by his red-brown cloak, but by the fact that his personal jewelry consisted only of a copper bracelet and a cloak pin with a jet head.

He had no idea how the time transition was to be made, nor how one might step from the polar regions of the Western Hemisphere to the island of Britain lying off the Eastern. And it was a complicated business as he discovered.

The transition itself was a fairly simple, though disturbing, process. One walked a short corridor and stood for an instant on a plate while the light centered there curled about in a solid core, shutting one off from floor and wall. Ross gasped for breath as the air was sucked out of his lungs. He experienced a moment of deathly sickness with the sensation of being lost in nothingness. Then he breathed again and looked through the dying wall of light to where Ashe waited.

Quick and easy as the trip through time had been,

the journey to Britain was something else. There could be only one transfer point if the secret was to be preserved. But men from that point must be moved swiftly and secretly to their appointed stations. Ross, knowing the strict rules concerning the transportation of objects from one time to another, wondered how that travel could be effected. After all, they could not spend months, or even years, getting across continents and seas.

The answer was ingenious. Three days after they had stepped through the barrier of time at the outpost, Ross and Ashe balanced on the rounded back of a whale. It was a whale which would deceive anyone who did not test its hide with a harpoon, and whalers with harpoons large enough to trouble such a monster were yet well in the future.

Ashe slid a dugout into the water, and Ross climbed into that unsteady craft, holding it against the side of the disguised sub until his partner joined him. The day, misty and drizzling, made the shore they aimed for a half-seen line across the water. With a shiver born of more than cold, Ross dipped his paddle and helped Ashe send their crude boat toward that half-hidden strip of land.

There was no real dawn; the sky lightened somewhat, but the drizzle continued. Green patches showed among the winter-denuded trees back from the beach, but the countryside facing them gave an impression of untamed wilderness. Ross knew from his briefing that the whole of Britain was as yet only sparsely settled. The first wave of hunter-fishers to establish villages had been joined by other invaders who built massive tombs and had an elaborate religion. Small village-forts had been linked from hill to hill by trackways. There were "factories," which turned out in bulk such fine flint weapons and tools that a thriving industry was in full operation, not yet having been superseded by the metal imported by the Beaker merchants. Bronze was still so rare and costly that only the head man of a village could hope to own one of the long daggers. Even the arrowheads in Ross's quiver were chipped of flint.

They drew the dugout well up onto the shore and ran it into a shallow depression in the bank, heaping stones and brush about for its concealment. Then Ashe intently surveyed the surrounding country, seeking a landmark.

"Inland from here . . . ." Ashe used the language of the Beakermen, and Ross knew that from now on he must not only live as a trader, but also think as one. All other memories must be buried under the false one he had learned; he must be interested in the present rate of exchange and the chance for profit. The two men were on their way to Outpost Gog, where Ashe's first partner, the redoubtable Sanford, was playing his role so well.

The rain squished in their hide boots, made sodden strings of their cloaks, plastered their woven caps to their thick mats of hair. Yet Ashe bore steadily on across the land with the certainty of one following a marked trail. His self-confidence was rewarded within the first half mile when they came out upon one of the link trackways, its beaten surface testifying to constant use.

Here Ashe turned eastward, stepping up the pace to a ground-covering trot. The peace of the road held— at least by day. By night only the most hardened and desperate outlaws would brave the harmful spirits roving in the dark.

All the lore that had been pounded into him at the

base began to make some sense to Ross as he followed his guide, sniffing strange wet smells from the brush, the trees, and the damp earth; piecing together in his mind what he had been taught and what he now saw for himself, until it made a tight pattern.

The track they were following sloped slightly upward, and a change in the wind brought to them a sour odor, blanking out all normal scents. Ashe halted so suddenly that Ross almost plowed into him. But he was alerted by the older man's attitude.

Something had been burned! Ross drew in a deep lungful of the smell and then wished that he had not. It was wood—burned wood—and something else. Since this was not possibly normal, he was prepared for the way Ashe melted into cover in the brush.

They worked their way, sometimes crawling on their bellies, through the wet stands of dead grass, taking full advantage of all cover. They crouched at the top of the hill while Ashe parted the prickly branches of an evergreen bush to make them a window.

The black patch left by the fire, which had come from a ruin above, had spread downhill on the opposite side of the valley. Charred posts still stood like lone teeth in a skull to mark what must have once been one of the stockade walls of a post. But all they now guarded was a desolation from which came that overpowering stench.

"Our post?" Ross asked in a whisper.

Ashe nodded. He was studying the scene with an intent absorption which, Ross knew, would impress every important detail upon his mind. That the place had been burned was clear from the first. But why and by whom was a problem vital to the two lurking in the brush.

It took them almost an hour to cross the valley—an hour of hiding, casting about, searching. They had made a complete circle of the destroyed post and Ashe stood in the shadow of a copse, rubbing clots of mud from his hands and frowning up at the charred posts.

"They weren't rushed. Of, if they were, the attacker covered their trail afterward—" Ross ventured.

The older man shook his head. "Tribesmen would not have muddled a trail if they had won. No, this was no regular attack. There have been no signs of a war party coming or leaving."

"Then what?" demanded Ross.

"Lightning for one thing—and we'd better hope it was that. Or—" Ashe's blue eyes were very cold and bleak, as cold and bleak as the countryside about them.

"Or—?" Ross dared to prompt him.

"Or we have made contact with the Reds in the wrong way!"

Ross's hand instinctively went to the dagger at his belt. Little help a dagger would be in an unequal struggle like this! They were only two in a thin web of men strung out through centuries of time with orders to seek out that which did not fit properly into the pattern of the past: to locate the enemy wherever in history or prehistory he had gone to earth. Had the Reds been searching, too, and was this first disaster their victory?

The time traders had their evidence when they at last ventured into what had been the heart of Outpost Gog. Ross, inexperienced as he was in such matters, could not mistake the signs of the explosion. There was a crater on the crown of the hill, and Ashe stood apart from it, eyeing the fragments about them—

scorched wood, blackened stone.

"The Reds?"

"It must have been. This damage was done by explosives."

It was clear why Outpost Gog could not report the disaster. The attack had destroyed their one link with the post on this time level; the concealed communicator had gone up with the blast.

"Eleven—" Ashe's finger tapped on the ornate buckle of his wide belt. "We have about ten days to stick it out," he added, "and it seems we may be able to use them to better advantage than just letting you learn how it feels to walk about some four thousand years before you were born. We have to find out—if we can—what happened here and why!"

Ross gazed at the mess. "Dig?" he asked.

"Some digging is indicated."

So they dug. Finally, black with charcoal smudges and sick with the evidences of death they had chanced upon, they collapsed on the cleanest spot they could find.

"They must have hit at night," Ashe said slowly. "Only at that time would they find everyone here. Men don't trust a night filled with ghosts, and our agents conform to local custom as usual. All of the post people could be erased with one bomb at night."

All except two of them had been true Beaker traders, including women and children. No Beaker trading post was large, and this one was unusually small. The attacker had wiped out some twenty people, eighteen of them innocent victims.

"How long ago?" Ross wanted to know.

"Maybe two days. And this attack came without any warning, or Sandy would have sent a message. He had no suspicions at all; his last reports were all routine, which means that if they were on to him—and they must have been, judging by the results—he was not even aware of it."

"What do we do now?"

Ashe looked at him. "We wash—no—" he corrected himself—"we don't! We go to Nodren's village. We are frightened, grief-stricken. We have found our kinsmen dead under strange circumstances. We ask questions of one to whom I am known as an inhabitant of this post."

So, covered with dirt, they walked along the trackway toward the neighboring village with a weariness they did not have to counterfeit.

The dog sighted or perhaps scented them first. It was a rough-coated beast, showing its fangs with a wolflike ferocity. But it was smaller than a wolf, and it barked between its warning snarls. Ashe brought his bow from beneath the shelter of his cloak and held it ready.

"Ho, one comes to speak with Nodren—Nodren of the Hill!"

Only the dog snapped and snarled. Ashe rubbed his forearm across his face, the gesture of a weary and heartsick man, smearing the ash and grime into an awesome mask.

"Who speaks to Nodren—?" There was a different twist to the pronunciation of some words, but Ross was able to understand.

"One who has hunted with him and feasted with him. The one who gave into his hand the friendship of the ever-sharp knife. It is Assha of the traders."

"Go far from us, man of ill luck. You who are hunted by the evil spirits." The last was a shrill cry.

Ashe remained where he was, facing into the bushes which hid the tribesman.

"Who speaks for Nodren yet not with the voice of Nodren?" he demanded. "This is Assha who asks. We have drunk blood together and faced the white wolf and the wild boar in their fury. Nodren lets not others speak for him, for Nodren is a man and a chief!"

"And you are cursed!" A stone flew through the air, striking a rain pool and spattering mud on Ashe's boots. "Go and take your evil with you!"

"Is it from the hand of Nodren or Nodren's young men that doom came upon those of my blood? Have war arrows passed between the place of the traders and the town of Nodren? Is that why you hide in the shadows so that I, Assha, cannot look upon the face of one who speaks boldly and throws stones?"

"No war arrows between us, trader. *We* do not provoke the spirits of the hills. No fire comes from the sky at night to eat us up with a noise of many thunders. Lurgha speaks in such thunders; Lurgha's hand smites with such fire. You have the wrath of Lurgha upon you, trader! Keep away from us lest Lurgha's wrath fall upon us also."

Lurgha was the local storm god, Ross recalled. The sound of thunder and fire coming out of the sky at night—the bomb! Perhaps the very method of attack on the post would defeat Ashe's attempt to learn anything from these neighbors. The superstitions of the people would lead them to shun both the site of the post and Ashe himself as cursed and taboo.

"If the Wrath of Lurgha had struck at Assha, would Assha still live to walk upon this road?" Ashe prodded the ground with the tip of his bowstave. "Yet Assha walks, as you see him; Assha talks, as you hear him. It is ridiculous to answer him with the nonsense of little children—"

"Spirits so walk and talk to unlucky men," retorted

the man in hiding. "It may be the spirt of Assha who does so now—"

Ashe made a sudden leap. There was a flurry of action behind the bush screen and he reappeared, dragging into the gray light of the rainy day a wriggling captive, whom he bumped without ceremony onto the beaten earth of the road.

The man was bearded, wearing his thick mop of black hair in a round topknot secured by a hide loop. He wore a skin tunic, now in considerable disarray, which was held in place with a woven, tasseled belt.

"Ho, so it is Lal of the Quick Tongue who speaks so loudly of spirits and the Wrath of Lurgha!" Ashe studied his captive. "Now, Lal, since you speak for Nodren—which I believe will greatly surprise him— you will continue to tell me of this Wrath of Lurgha from the night skies and what has happened to Sanfra, who was my brother, and those others of my kin. I am Assha, and you know of the wrath of Assha and how it ate up Twist-tooth, the outlaw, when he came in with his evil men. The Wrath of Lurgha is hot, but so too is the wrath of Assha." Ashe contorted his face in such a way that Lal squirmed and looked away. When the tribesman spoke, all his former authority and bluster had gone.

"Assha knows that I am his dog. Let him not turn upon me his swift-cutting big knife, nor the arrows from his lightning bow. It was the Wrath of Lurgha which smote the place on the hill, first the thunder of his fist meeting the earth, and then the fire which he breathed upon those whom he would slay—"

"And this you saw with your own eyes, Lal?"

The shaggy head shook an emphatic negative. "Assha knows that Lal is no chief who can stand and look upon the wonders of Lurgha's might and keep his eyes in his head. Nodren himself saw this wonder—"

"And if Lurgha came in the night, when all men keep to their homes and leave the outer world to the restless spirits, how did Nodren see his coming?"

Lal crouched lower to the ground, his eyes darting to the bushes and the freedom they promised, then back to Ashe's firmly planted boots.

"I am not a chief, Assha. How could I know in what way or for what reason Nodren saw the coming of Lurgha—?"

"Fool!" A second voice, that of a woman, spat the word from the brush which fringed the roadway. "Speak to Assha with a straight tongue. If he is a spirit, he will know that you do not tell him the truth. And if he has been spared by Lurgha . . ." She showed her wonderment with a hiss of indrawn breath.

So urged, Lal mumbled sullenly, "It is said that there came a message for one to witness the Wrath of Lurgha in its descent upon the outlanders so that Nodren and the men of Nodren would truly know that the traders were cursed, and should be put to the spear should they come here again—"

"This message—how was it brought? Did the voice of Lurgha sound in Nodren's ear alone, or came it by the tongue of some man?"

"Ahee!" Lal lay flat on the ground, his hands over his ears.

"Lal is a fool and fears his own shadow as it skips before him on a sunny day!" Out of the bushes stepped a young woman, obviously of some importance in her own group. Walking with a proud stride, her eyes boldly met Ashe's. A shining disk hung about her neck on a thong, and another decorated the woven belt of her cloth tunic. Her hair was bound in a thread net fastened with jet pins.

"I greet Cassca, who is the First Sower." There was a formal note in Ashe's voice. "But why should Cassca hide from Assha?"

"There has been death on your hill, Assha—" she sniffed—"you smell of it now—Lurgha's death. Those who come from that hill may well be some who no longer walk in their bodies." Cassca placed her fingers momentarily on Ashe's outstretched palm before she nodded. "No spirit are you, Assha, for all know that a spirit is solid to the eye, but not to the touch. So it would seem that you were not burned up by Lurgha, after all."

"This matter of a message from Lurgha—" he prompted.

"It came out of the empty air in the hearing not only of Nodren, but also of Hangor, Effar, and myself, Cassca. For we stood at that time near the Old Place . . ." She made a curious gesture with the fingers of her right hand. "It will soon be the time of sowing, and though Lurgha brings sun and rain to feed the grain, yet it is in the Great Mother that the seed lies. Upon her business only women may go into the Inner Circle." She gestured again. "But as we met to make the first sacrifice there came music out of the air such as we have never heard, voices singing like birds in a strange tongue." Her face assumed an awesome expression. "Afterward a voice said that Lurgha was angered with the hill of the men-from-afar and that in the night he would send his Wrath against them, and that Nodren must witness this thing so that he could see what Lurgha did to those he would punish. So it was done by Nodren. And there was a sound in the air—"

"What kind of a sound?" Ashe asked quietly.

"Nodren said it was a hum and there was the dark shadow of Lurgha's bird between him and the stars. Then came the smiting of the hill with thunder and lightning, and Nodren fled, for the Wrath of Lurgha is a fearsome thing. Now do the people to the Great Mother's Place with many fine offerings that she may stand between them and that Wrath."

"Assha thanks Cassca, who is the handmaiden of the Great Mother. May the sowing prosper and the reaping be good this year!" Ashe said finally, ignoring Lal, who still groveled on the road.

"You go from this place, Assha?" she asked. "For though I stand under the protecting hand of the Mother and so do not fear, yet there are others who will raise their spears against you for the honor of Lurgha."

"We go, and again thanks be to you, Cassca."

He turned back the way they had come, and Ross fell in beside him as the woman watched them out of sight.

6

"THAT BIRD of Lurgha's—" said Ross, once they were out of sight of Cassca and Lal, "could it have been a plane?"

"Sounds like it," snapped his companion. "If the Reds have done their work efficiently, and there's no reason to suppose otherwise, then there is no use in contacting either Dorhta's town or Munga's. The same announcement concerning the Wrath of Lurgha was probably made there—to their good purpose, not ours."

"Cassca didn't seem to be overly impressed with Lurgha's curse, not as much as the man was."

"She is the closest thing to a priestess that this tribe knows, and she serves a goddess older and more powerful than Lurgha—the Mother Earth, the Great Mother, goddess of fertility and growth. Nodren's people believe that unless Cassca performs her mysteries and sows part of the first field in the spring there won't be any harvest. Consequently, she is secure in her office and doesn't fear the Wrath of

Lurgha too much. These people are now changing from one type of worship to another, but some of Cassca's beliefs will persist clear down to our day, taking on the coating of 'magic' and a lot of other enameling along the way."

Ashe had been talking as a man talks to cover up furious thinking. Now he paused again and turned toward the sea. "We have to stick it out somewhere until the sub comes to pick us up. We'll need shelter."

"Will the tribesmen be after us?"

"They may well be. Let the right men get to talking up a holy extermination of those upon whom the Wrath of Lurgha has fallen and we could be in for plenty of trouble. Some of those men are trained hunters and trackers, and the Reds may have planted an agent to report the return of anyone to our post. Just now we're about the most important time travelers out, for we know the Reds have appeared on this line. They must have a large post here, too, or they couldn't have sent a plane on that raid. You can't build a time transport large enough to take through a considerable amount of material. Everything used by us in this age has to be assembled on this side, and the use of all machines is limited to where they can not be seen by any natives. Luckily large sections of this world are mostly wilderness and unpopulated in the areas where we operate the base posts. So if the Reds have a plane, it was put together here, and that means a big post somewhere." Again Ashe was thinking aloud as he pushed ahead of Ross into the fringes of a wood. "Sandy and I scouted this territory pretty well last spring. There is a cave about half a mile to the west; it will shelter us for tonight."

Ashe's plans would probably have been easily accomplished if the cave had been unoccupied. Without incident they came down into a hollow through which trickled a small stream, its banks laced with a thin edging of ice. Under Ashe's direction Ross collected an armload of firewood. He was no woodsman and his prolonged exposure to the chilling drizzle made him eager for even the very rough shelter of a cave, so eager that he plunged forward carelessly. His foot came down on a slippery patch of mud, sending him sprawling on his face. There was a growl, and a white bulk rushed him. The cloak, rucked up about his throat and shoulders, then saved his life, for only stout cloth was caught between those fangs.

With a startled cry, Ross rolled as he might have to escape a man's attack, struggling to unsheath his dagger. A white-hot flash of pain scored his upper arm. The breath was driven out of him as a fight raged over his prone body; he heard grunts, snarls, and was severely pommeled. Then he was free as the bodies broke away. Shaken, he got to his knees. A short distance away the fight was still in progress. He saw Ashe straddle the body of a huge white wolf, his legs clamped about the animal's haunches, his hooked arm under the beast's head, forcing it up and back while his dagger rose and sank twice in the underparts of the heaving body.

Ross held his own weapon ready. He leaped from a half crouch, and his dagger sank cleanly home behind the short ribs. One of their blows must have reached the animal's heart. With an almost human cry the wolf stiffened convulsively. Then it was still. Ashe squatted near it, methodically driving his dagger into the moist soil to clean the blade.

A red rivulet trickled down his thigh where the lower edge of his kilt-tunic had been ripped up to the link belt. He was breathing hard, but otherwise he was as composed as always. "These sometimes hunt in pairs at this season," he observed. "Be ready with your bow—"

Ross strung his with the cord he had been keeping dry within the breast folds of his tunic. He fitted an arrow to the string, grateful to be a passable marksman. The slash on his arm smarted in protest as he moved, and he noted that Ashe did not try to get up.

"A bad one?" Ross indicated the blood now thickening into a stream along Ashe's thigh.

Ashe pulled away the torn tunic and exposed a nasty looking gash on the outside of his hip. He pressed his palm against the gaping wound and motioned Ross to scout ahead. "See if the cave is clear. We can't do anything until we know that."

Reluctantly Ross followed the stream until he found the cave, a snug-looking place with an overhang to keep it dry. The unpleasant smell of a lair hung about its mouth. He chose a stone from the stream, chucked it into the dark opening, and waited. The stone rattled as it struck an inner wall, but there was no other sound. A second stone from a different angle followed the first, with the same results. Ross was now certain that the cave was unoccupied. Once they were inside with a fire going at the entrance, they could hope to keep it free of intruders. A little heartened, he cast about a bit upstream and then turned back to where he had left Ashe.

"No male?" the other greeted him. "This is a female, and she was close to whelping—" He nudged the white wolf with his toe. His hands held a pad of rags against his hip, and his face was shaded with pain.

"Nothing in the cave anyway. Let's see about

this . . ." Ross laid aside the bow and kneeled to examine Ashe's thigh wound. His own slash was more of a smarting graze, but this tear was deep and ugly.

"Second plate—belt—" Ashe got the words out between set teeth, and Ross clicked open the hidden recess in the other's bronze belt to bring out a small packet. Ashe made a wry face as he swallowed three of the pills within. Ross mashed another pill onto the bandage he prepared, and when the last cumbersome fold was secure Ashe relaxed.

"Let us hope that works," he commented a little bleakly. "Now come here where I can get my hands on you and let me see your scratch. Animal bites can be a nasty business."

Bandaged in turn, with the bitterness of an antisepto pill on his tongue, Ross helped Ashe limp upstream to the cave. He left the older man outside while he cleaned up the floor of the cave and then made his companion as comfortable as he could on a bed of bracken. The fire Ross had longed for was built. They stripped off their sodden clothing and hung it to dry. Ross wrapped a bird he had shot in clay and tucked it under the hot coals to be roasted.

They had surely had bad luck, he thought, but they were now undercover, had a fire, and food of a sort. His arm ached, sharp pain shooting from fingers to elbow when he moved it. Though Ashe made no complaint, Ross gauged that the older man's discomfort was far worse than his own, and he carefully hid all signs of his own twinges.

They ate the bird, saltless, and with their fingers. Ross savored each greasy bit, licking his hands clean afterward while Ashe lay back on the improvised bed, his face gaunt in the half light of the fire.

"We are about five miles from the sea here. There

is no way of raising our base now that Sandy's installation is gone. I'll have to lay up, since I can't risk any more loss of blood. And you're not too good in the woods—"

Ross accepted that valuation with a new humbleness. He was only too well aware that if it had not been for Ashe, he and not the white wolf would have died down in the valley. Yet a strange shyness kept him from trying to put his thanks into words. The only kind of amends he could make for the other's hurt was to provide hands, feet, and strength for the man who did know what to do and how to do it.

"We'll have to hunt—" he ventured.

"Deer," Ashe caught him up. "But the marsh at the mouth of this stream provides a better hunting ground than inland. If the wolf laired here very long, she has already frightened away any large game. It isn't the matter of food which bothers me—"

"It is being tied up here," Ross filled in for him with some daring. "But look here, I'll take orders. This is your territory, and I'm green at the game. You tell me what to do, and I'll do it the best that I can." He glanced up to find Ashe surveying him intently, but as usual there was no readable expression on the other's brown face.

"The first thing to do is get the wolf's hide," Ashe said briskly. "Then bury the carcass. You'd better drag it up here to work on it. If her mate is hanging around, he might try to jump you."

Why Ashe should think it necessary to acquire the wolf skin puzzled Ross, but he asked no questions. His skinning task took four times as long and was far from being the neat job the shock-haired man of the record tape had accomplished. Ross had to wash himself off in the stream before piling stones over the corpse in temporary burial. When he pulled his bloody burden back to the cave, Ashe lay with his eyes closed. Ross thankfully sat on his own pile of bracken and tried not to notice the throbbing ache in his arm.

He must have fallen asleep, for when he roused it was to see Ashe crawl over to mend the dying fire from their store of wood. Ross, angry at himself, beat the other to the task.

"Get back," he said roughly. "This is my job. I didn't mean to fail."

Surprisingly, Ashe settled back without a word, leaving Ross to sit by the fire, a fire he was very glad to have a moment or so later when a wailing howl sounded down-wind. If this was not the white wolf's mate, then it was another of her kin who prowled the upper reaches of the small valley.

The next day, having provided Ashe with a supply of firewood, Ross went to try his luck in the marsh. The thick drizzle which had hung over the land the day before was gone, and he faced a clear, bright morning, though the breeze had an icy snap. But it was a good morning to be alive and out in the open, and Ross's spirits rose.

He tried to put to use all the woodlore he had learned at the base. But it was one thing to learn something academically and another to put that learning into practice. He was uncomfortably certain that Ashe would not have found his showing very good.

The marsh was a series of pools between rank growths of leafless willows and coarse tufts of grass, with hillocks of firmer soil rising like islands. Ross, approaching with caution, was glad of it, for from one of those hillocks arose a trail of white smoke, and he saw a black blot which was probably a rude hut. Why one should choose to live in the midst of such country he could not guess, though it might be merely the temporary camp of some hunter.

Ross also saw thousands of birds feeding greedily on the dried seed of the marsh grasses, paddling in the pools, and setting up a clamor to drive a man mad. They did not seem in the least disturbed by that distant camper.

Ross had reason to be proud of his marksmanship that morning. He had in his quiver perhaps half a dozen of the lighter shafts made for shooting birds. In place of the finely chipped and wickedly barbed flint points used for heavier game, these were tipped with needle-sharp, light bone heads. He had a string of four birds looped together by their feet within almost as many minutes. For the flocks rose in their first alarm only to settle again to feast.

Then he knocked over a hare—a fat giant of its race —that stared at him brazenly from a tussock. The hare kicked back into a pool in its death struggle, however, and Ross was forced to leave cover to retrieve its body. But he was alert and he stood up, dagger out and ready, to greet the man who parted the bushes to watch him.

For a long minute gray eyes stared into brown ones, and then Ross noted the other's bedraggled and tattered dress. The kilt-tunic smudged with mud, scorched and charred along one edge, was styled like his own. The fellow wore his hair fastened back with a band, unlike the topknot of the local tribesman.

Ross, his dagger still ready, broke the silence first. "I am a believer in the fire and the fashioned metal, the climbing sun, and the moving water." He repeated the recognition speech of the Beakermen.

"The fire warms by the grace of Tulden, the metal is fashioned by the mystery of the smith, the sun climbs without our aid, and who can stop the water from running?" The stranger's voice was hoarse. Now that Ross had time to examine him more closely he saw the dark bruise on his exposed shoulder, the raw red mark of a burn running across the man's broad chest. He dared to test his surmise concerning the other.

"I am the kin of Assha. We returned to the hill—"

"Ashe!"

Not "Assha" but "Ashe!" Ross, though sure of that pronunciation, was still cautious. "You are from the hill place, where Lurgha smote with thunder and fire?"

The man slid his long legs across the log which had been his shelter. The burn across his chest was not his only brand, for Ross noticed another red stripe, puffed and fiery looking, which swelled the calf of one leg. The man studied Ross closely, and then his fingers moved in a sign which to the uninitiated native might have been one for the warding off of evil, but which to Ross was the "thumbs up" of his own age.

"Sanford?"

At that name the man shook his head. "McNeil," he named himself. "Where is Ashe?"

He might really be what he seemed, but on the other hand, he could be a Red spy. Ross had not forgotten Kurt. "What happened?" he parried one question with another.

"Bomb. The Reds must have spotted us, and we didn't have a chance. We weren't expecting any trouble. I'd been down to see about a missing burden donkey and was about halfway back up the hill when she hit. When I came to I was all the way down the

hill with part of the fort on top of me. The rest . . .
Well, you saw the place, didn't you?"

Ross nodded. "What are you doing here?"

McNeil spread his hands in a tired little gesture. "I
tried to talk to Nodren, but they stoned me away. I
knew that Ashe was coming through and hoped to
reach him when he hit the beach, but I was too late.
Then I figured he would pass here to make contact
with the sub, so I was waiting it out until I saw you.
Where is Ashe?"

It all sounded logical enough. Still, with Ashe injured, Ross was taking no chances. He pushed his
dagger back into its sheath and picked up the hare.
"Stay here," he told McNeil, "I'll be back—"

"But—wait! Where's Ashe, you young fool? We
have to get together."

Ross went on. He was sure that the stranger was in
no shape to race after him, and he would lay a muddled trail before he returned to the cave valley. If this
man was a Red plant, he would have to reckon with
one who had already met Kurt Vogel.

The laying of that muddled trail took time. It was
past midday when Ross came back to Ashe, who was
sitting up by the mouth of the cave at the fire, using
his dagger to fashion a crutch out of a length of sapling. He surveyed Ross's burden with approval, but
lost interest in the promise of food as soon as the other reported his meeting in the marsh.

"McNeil—chap with brown hair, brown eyes, a
right eyebrow which quirks up toward his hairline
when he smiles?"

"Brown hair and eyes, okay—and he didn't smile
any."

"Chip broken off a front tooth—upper right?"

Ross shut his eyes to visualize the stranger. Yes,

there had been a small break on a front tooth. He nodded.

"That's McNeil. Not that you didn't do right not to bring him here without being sure. What made you so watchful? Kurt?"

Again Ross nodded. "And what you said about the Reds' planting someone here to wait for us."

Ashe scratched the bristles on his chin. "Never underrate them—we don't dare do that. But the man you met is McNeil, and we'd better get him here. Can you bring him?"

"I think he's able to get about, in spite of that leg. From his story he's been stirring around."

Ashe bit absent-mindedly into a piece of hare and swore mildly when he burned his tongue. "Odd that Cassca didn't tell us about him. Unless she thought there was no use causing trouble by admitting they had driven him away. You going now?"

Ross moved around the fire. "Might as well. He didn't look too comfortable. And I'll bet he's hungry."

He took the direct route back to the marsh, but this time no thread of smoke spiraled into the air. Ross hesitated. That shelter on the small island was surely the place where McNeil had holed up. Should he try to work his way out to it now? Or had something happened to the man while he was gone?

Again that sixth sense of impending disaster, which is perhaps bred into some men, alerted Ross. Why he turned suddenly and backed against a bushy willow, he could not have explained. However, because he did so the loop of hide rope meant for his throat hit his shoulder harmlessly. It fell to the ground, and he stamped one boot down on it. Then it was the work of seconds to grasp it and give it a quick jerk. The surprised man who held the other end was brought sprawling into the open.

Ross had seen that round face before. "Lal of the town of Nodren." He found words to greet the ropeman even as his knee came up against the fellow's jaw, jarring Lal so that he dropped a flint knife. Ross kicked it into the willows. "What do you hunt here, Lal?"

"Traders!" The voice was weak, but it held heat.

The tribesman did not try to struggle against Ross's hold, and Ross, gripping him by the nape of the neck, moved through a screen of brush to a hollow. Luckily there was no water cupped there, for McNeil lay in the bottom of that dip, his arms tied tightly behind him and his ankles lashed together with no thought for the pain of his burned leg.

7

ROSS WHIRLED the rope which had been meant to bring him down around Lal. He lashed the tribesman's arms tight to his body before he knelt to cut loose his fellow time traveler. Lal now huddled against the far wall of the cup, fear in every line of his small body. So apparent was this fear that Ross felt no satisfaction at turning the tables on him. Instead he felt increasingly uneasy.

"What is this all about?" he asked McNeil as he stripped off his bonds and helped him up.

McNeil massaged his wrists, took a step or two, and grimaced with pain. "Our friend seeks to be an obedient servant of Lurgha."

Ross picked up his bow. "The tribe is out to hunt us?"

"Lurgha has ordered—out of thin air again—that any traders who escaped are to be brought in and introduced to him personally at the sacrifice for the enrichment of the fields!"

The old, old gift of blood and life at the spring sowing. Ross recalled grisly details from his cram lessons. Any wandering stranger or enemy tribesman taken in a raid before that day would meet such a fate. On unlucky years when people were not available a deer or wolf might serve. But the best sacrifice of all was a man. So Lurgha had decreed—from the air—that traders were his meat? What of Ashe? Let any hunter from the village track him down.

"We have to move fast," Ross told McNeil as he took up the rope which made a leading cord for Lal. Ashe would want to question the tribesman about this second order from Lurgha.

Impatient as Ross was, he had to mend his pace to accommodate McNeil. The man from the hill post was close to the end of his strength. He had started off bravely enough, but now he wavered. Ross sent Lal ahead with a sharp push, ordering him to stay there, while he went to McNeil's aid. It was well into the afternoon before they came up the stream and saw the fire before the cave.

"Macna!" Ashe hailed Ross's companion with the native version of his name. "And Lal. But what do you here, Lal of Nodren's town?"

"Mischief." Ross helped McNeil within the cave and to the pile of brush which was his own bed. "He was hunting traders as a present for Lurgha."

"So—" Ashe turned upon the tribesman—"and by whose word did you go hunting my kinsman, Lal? Was it Nodren's? Has he forgotten the blood bond between us? For it was in the name of Lurgha himself that that bond was made—"

"Aaaah—" The tribesman squatted down against the wall where Ross had shoved him. Unable to hide his head in his arms, he brought his face down upon his knees so that only his shaggy topknot of hair was

exposed. Ross realized, with stupefaction, that the little man was crying like a child, his hunched shoulders
rising and falling with the force of his sobs.

"Aaaah—" he wailed.

Ashe allowed him a moment or two of noisy grief
and then limped over to grasp his topknot and pull up
his head. Lal's eyes were screwed tightly shut, but
there were tears on his cheeks, and his mouth twisted
in another wail.

"Be quiet!" Ashe shook him, but not too harshly.
"Have you yet felt the bite of my sharp knife? Has an
arrow holed your skin? You are alive, and you could
be dead. Show that you are glad you live and continue
to breathe by telling us what you know, Lal."

The woman Cassca had displayed a measure of intelligence and ease at their meeting upon the road.
But it was very plain that Lal was of different stuff, a
simple man in whose head few ideas could find house
room at one time. And to him the present was all
black. Little by little they dragged the story out of
him.

Lal was poor, so poor that he had never dared
dream of owning for himself some of the precious
things the hill traders displayed to the wealthy of
Nodren's town. But he was also a follower of the
Great Mother's, rather than one who made sacrifices
to Lurgha. Lurgha was the god for warriors and great
men; he was too high to concern himself with such as
Lal.

So when Nodren reported the end of the hill post
under the storm fist of Lurgha, Lal had been impressed only to a point. He was still convinced it was
none of his concern, and instead he began thinking of
the treasures which might lie hidden in the destroyed
buildings. It occurred to him that Lurgha's Wrath

had been laid upon the men who had owned them, but perhaps it would not stretch to the fine things themselves. So he had gone secretly to the hill to explore.

What he had seen there had utterly converted him to a belief in the fury of Lurgha and he had been frightened out of his simple wits, fleeing without making the search he had intended. But Lurgha had seen him there, had read his impious thoughts . . .

At that point Ashe interrupted the stream of Lal's story. How had Lurgha seen Lal?

Because—Lal shuddered, began to cry again, and spoke the next few sentences haltingly—that very morning when he had gone out to hunt wild fowl in the marshes Lurgha had spoken to *him,* to Lal, who was less than a flea creeping upon a wornout fur rug.

And how had Lurgha spoken? Ashe's voice was softer, gentle.

Out of the air, even as he had spoken to Nodren, who was a chief. He said that he had seen Lal in the hill post, and so Lal was his meat. But not yet would he eat him, not if Lal served him in other ways. And he, Lal, had lain flat on the ground before the bodiless voice of Lurgha and had sworn that he would serve Lurgha to the end of his life.

Then Lurgha had told him to hunt down one of the evil traders who was hiding in the marshes, and bind him with ropes. Then he was to call the men of the village and together they would carry the prisoner to the hill where Lurgha had loosed his wrath, and there they would leave him. Later they might return and take what they found there and use it to bless the fields at sowing time, and all would be well with Nodren's village. And Lal had sworn that he would do as Lurgha bade, but now he could not. So Lurgha would eat him up—he was a man without hope.

"Yet," Ashe said even more gently, "have you not served the Great Mother all these years, giving to her a portion of the first fruits even when the yield of your one field was small?"

Lal stared at him, his woebegone face still smeared with tears. It took a second or two for the question to penetrate his fear-clouded mind. Then he nodded timidly.

"Has she not dealt with you well in return, Lal? You are a poor man, that is true, But you are not gaunt of belly, even though this is the thin season when men fast before coming of the new harvest. The Great Mother watches over her own. And it is she who has brought you to us now. For this I say to you, Lal, and I, Assha of the traders, speak with a straight tongue. The Lurgha who struck our post, who spoke to you from the air, means you no good—"

"Aaaah!" wailed Lal. "So do I know, Assha. He is of the blackness and the wandering spirits of the dark!"

"Just so. Thus he is no kin to the Mother, for she is of the light and of good things, of the new grain, and the newborn lambs for your flocks, of the maids who wed with men and bring forth sons to lift their fathers' spears, daughters to spin by the hearth and sow the yellow grain in the furrows. Lurgha's quarrel lies with us, Lal, not with Nodren nor with you. And we take upon us that quarrel." He limped into the outer air where the shadows of evening were beginning to creep across the ground.

"Hear me, Lurgha," he called into the coming night, "I am Assha of the traders, and upon myself I take your hate. Not upon Lal, nor upon Nodren, nor upon the people who live in Nodren's town, shall your wrath lie. Thus do I say it!"

Ross, noticing that Ashe concealed from Lal a wave of his hand, was prepared for some display meant to impress the tribesman. It came in a spectacular burst of green fire beyond the stream. Lal wailed again, but when that fire was followed by no other manifestation he ventured to raise his head once more.

"You have seen how Lurgha answered me, Lal. Toward me only will his wrath be turned. Now—" Ashe limped back and dragged out the white wolf skin, dropping it before Lal—"this you will give to Cassca that she may make a curtain for the Mother's home. See, it is white and so rare that the Mother will be pleased with such a fine gift. And you will tell her all that has chanced and how you believe in her powers over the powers of Lurgha, and the Mother will be well pleased with you. But you shall say nothing to the men of the village, for this quarrel is between Lurgha and Assha now and not for the meddling of others."

He unfastened the rope which bound Lal's arms. Lal reached out a hand to the wolf skin, his eyes filled with wonderment. "This is a fine thing you give me, Assha, and the Mother will be pleased, for in many years she has not had such a curtain for her secret place. Also, I am but a little man; the quarrels of great ones are not for me. Since Lurgha has accepted your words this is none of my affair. Yet I will not go back to the village for a while—with your permission, Assha. For I am a man of loose and wagging tongue and oftentimes I speak what I do not really wish to say. So if I am asked questions, I answer. If I am not there to be asked such questions, I cannot answer."

McNeil laughed, and Ashe smiled. "Well enough,

Lal. Perhaps you are a wiser man than you think. But also I do not believe you should stay here."

The tribesman was already nodding. "That do I say, too, Assha. You are now facing the Wrath of Lurgha, and with that I wish no part. Thus I shall go into the marsh for a while. There are birds and hares to hunt, and I shall work upon this fine skin so that when I take it to the Mother it shall indeed be a gift worth her smiles. Now, Assha, I would go before the night comes if it pleases you."

"Go with good fortune, Lal." Ashe stood apart while the tribesman ducked his head in a shy, awkward farewell to the others, pattering out into the valley.

"What if they pick him up?" McNeil asked wearily.

"I don't think they can," Ashe returned. "And what would you do—keep him here? If we tried that, he'd scheme to escape and try to turn the tables on us. Now he'll keep away from Nodren's village and out of sight for the time being. Lal's not too bright in some ways, but he's a good hunter. If he has reason for hiding out, it'll take a better hunter to track him. At least we know now that the Reds are afraid they did not make a clean sweep here. What happened, McNeil?"

While he was telling his story in more detail both Ashe and Ross worked on his burns, making him comfortable. Then Ashe sat back as Ross prepared food.

"How did they spot the post?" Ashe rubbed his chin and frowned at the fire.

"Only way I can guess is that they picked up our post signal and pinpointed the source. That means they must have been hunting us for some time."

"No strangers about lately?"

McNeil shook his head. "Our cover wasn't broken that way. Sanford was a wonder. If I hadn't known better, I would have sworn he was born one of the Beaker folk. He had a network of informants running all the way from here into Brittany. Amazing how he was able to work without arousing any suspicions. I suppose his being a member of the smiths' guild was a big help. He could pick up a lot of news from any village where there was one at work. And I tell you," McNeil propped himself up on his elbow to exclaim more vehemently—"there wasn't a whisper of trouble from here clear across the channel and pretty far to the north. We were already sure the south was clean before we ever took cover as Beakers, especially since their clans are thick in Spain."

Ashe chewed a broiled wing reflectively. "Their permanent base with the transport *has* to be somewhere within the bounds of the territory they hold in our own time."

"They could plant it in Siberia and laugh at us," McNeil exploded. "No hope of getting in there—"

"No." Ashe threw the stripped bone into the fire and licked grease from his fingers. "Then they would be faced with the old problem of distance. If what they are exploiting lay within their modern boundaries, we would never have tumbled to the thing in the first place. What the Reds want must lie outside their twentieth century holdings, a slender point in our favor. Therefore they will plant their shift point as close to it as they can. Our transportation problem is more difficult than theirs will ever be.

"You know why we chose the arctic for our base; it lies in a section of the world never populated by other than roving hunters. But I'll wager anything you want to name that their point is somewhere in Europe where they have people to contend with. If they are using a plane, they can't risk its being seen—"

"I don't see why not," Ross broke in. "These people couldn't possibly know what it was—Lurgha's bird—magic—"

Ashe shook his head. "They must have the interference-with-history worry as much as we have. Anything of our own time has to be hidden or disguised in such a way that the native who may stumble upon it will never know it is manmade. Our sub is a whale to all appearances. Possibly their plane is a bird, but neither can bear too close an examination. We don't know what could result from a leak of real knowledge in this or any primitive time . . . how it might change history—"

"But," Ross advanced what he believed to be the best argument against that reasoning, "suppose I handed Lal a gun and taught him to use it. He couldn't duplicate the weapon—the technology required lies so far beyond his age. These people couldn't reproduce such a thing."

"True enough. On the other hand, don't belittle the ingenuity of the smiths or the native intelligence of men in any era. These tribesmen might not be able to reproduce your gun, but it would set them thinking along new lines. We might find that they would think our time right out of being. No, we dare not play tricks with the past. That is the same situation we faced immediately after the discovery of the atom bomb. Everybody raced to produce that new weapon and then sat around and shivered for fear we'd be crazy enough to use it on each other.

"The Reds have made new discoveries which we have to match, or we will go under. But back in time we have to be careful, both of us, or perhaps destroy the world we *do* live in."

"What do we do now?" McNeil wanted to know.

"Murdock and I came here only for a trial run. It's his test. The sub is to call for us about nine days from now."

"So if we sit tight—if we *can* sit tight—" McNeil lay down again—"they will take us out. Meanwhile we have nine days."

They spent three more days in the cave. McNeil was on his feet and impatient to leave before Ashe was able to hobble well enough to travel. Though Ross and McNeil took turns at hunting and guard duty, they saw no signs that the tribesmen were tracking them. Apparently Lal had done as he promised, withdrawing to the marsh and hiding there apart from his people.

In the gray of pre-dawn on the fourth day Ashe wakened Ross. Their fire had been buried with earth, and already the cave seemed bleak. They ate venison roasted the night before and went out into the chill of a fog. A little way down the valley McNeil joined them out of the mist from his guard post. Keeping their pace to one which favored Ashe's healing wound, they made their way inland in the direction of the track linking the villages.

Crossing that road they continued northward, the land beginning to rise under them. Far away they heard the blatting of sheep, the bark of a dog. In the fog, Ross stumbled in a shallow ditch beyond which lay a stubbled field. Ashe paused to look about him, his nostrils expanding as if he were a hound smelling out their trail.

The three went on, crossing a whole series of small, irregular fields. Ross was sure that the yield from any of these cleared strips must be scanty. The fog was thickening. Ashe pressed the pace, using his hand-made crutch carefully. He gave an audible sigh of relief when they were faced at last by two stone monoliths rising like pillars. A third stone lay across them, forming a rude arch through which they saw a narrow valley running back into the hills.

Through the fog Ross could sense the eerie strangeness of the valley beyond the massive gate. He would have said that he was not superstitious, that he had merely studied these tribal beliefs as lessons; he had not accepted them. Yet now, if he had been alone, he would have avoided that place and turned aside from the valley, for that which waited within was not for him. To his secret relief Ashe paused by the arch to wait.

The older man gestured the other two into cover. Ross obeyed willingly, though the dank drops of condensing fog dripped on his cloak and wet his face as he brushed against prickly-leafed shrubs. Here were walls of evergreen plants and dwarfed pines almost as if this tunnel of year-round greenery had been planted with some purpose in mind. Once his companions had concealed themselves, Ashe called, shrill but sweetly, with a bird's rising notes. Three times he made that sound before a figure moved in the fog, the rough gray-white of its long cloak melting in the wisps of mist.

Down that green tunnel, out of the heart of the valley, the other came, a loop of cloak concealing the entire figure. It halted right in back of the arch and Ashe, making a gesture to the others to stay where they were, faced the muffled stranger.

"Hands and feet of the Mother, she who sows what may be reaped—"

"Outland stranger who is under the Wrath of Lurgha," the other mocked him in the voice of Cassca. "What do you want, outlander, that you dare to come here where no man may enter?"

"That which you know. For on the night when Lurgha came you also saw—"

Ross heard the hiss of a sharply drawn breath. "How knew you that, outlander?"

"Because you serve the Mother and you are jealous for her and her service. If Lurgha is a mighty god, you wanted to see his acts with your own eyes."

When she finally answered, there was anger as well as frustration in her voice. "And you know of my shame then, Assha. For Lurgha came—on a bird he came, and he did even as he said he would. So now the village will make offerings to Lurgha and beg his favor, and the Mother will no more have those to harken to her words and offer her the first fruits of—"

"But from whence came this bird which was Lurgha, can you tell me that, she who waits upon the Mother?"

"What difference does it make from what direction Lurgha came? That does not add nor take from his power." Cassca moved beneath the arch. "Or does it in some strange way, Assha?"

"Perhaps it does. Only tell me."

She turned slowly and pointed over her right shoulder. "From that way he came, Assha. Well did I watch, knowing that I was the Mother's and that even Lurgha's thunderbolts could not eat me up. Does knowing that make Lurgha smaller in your eyes, Assha? When he has eaten up all that is yours and your kin with it?"

"Perhaps," Assha repeated. "I do not think Lurgha will come so again."

She shrugged, and the heavy cloak flapped. "That shall be as it shall be, Assha. Now go, for it is not good that any man come hither."

Cassca paced back into the heart of the green tunnel, and Ross and McNeil came out of concealment. McNeil faced in the direction she had pointed. "Northeast—" he commented thoughtfully, "the Baltic lies in that quarter."

8

". . . AND THAT is about all." Ten days later Ashe, a dressing on his leg and a few of the pain lines smoothed from his face, sat on a bunk in the arctic time post nursing a mug of coffee in his hands and smiling, a little crookedly, at Nelson Millaird.

Millaird, Kelgarries, Dr. Webb, all the top brass of the project had not only come through the transfer point to meet the three from Britain but were now crammed into the room, nearly pushing Ross and McNeil through the wall. Because this was it! What they had hunted for months—years—now lay almost within their grasp.

Only Millaird, the director, did not seem so confident. A big man with a bushy thatch of coarse graying hair and a heavy, fleshy face, he did not look like a brain. Yet Ross had been on the roster long enough to know that it was Millaird's thick and hairy hands that gathered all the loose threads of Operation Retrograde and deftly wove them into a workable pattern. Now the director leaned back in a chair which was too small for his bulk, chewing thoughtfully on a toothpick.

"So we have the first whiff of a trail," he commented without elation.

"A pretty strong lead!" Kelgarries broke in. Too excited to sit still, the major stood with his back against the door, as alert as if he were about to turn and face the enemy. "The Reds wouldn't have moved against Gog if they did not consider it a menace to them. Their big base must be in this time sector!"

"A big base," Millaird corrected. "The one we are after, no. And right now they may be switching times. Do you think they will sit here and wait for us to show up in force?" But Millaird's tone, intended to deflate, had no effect on the major.

"And just how long would it take them to dismantle a big base?" that officer countered. "At least a month. If we shoot a team in there in a hurry—"

Millaird folded his huge hands over his barrel-shaped body and laughed, without a trace of humor. "Just where do we send that team, Kelgarries? Northeast of a coastal point in Britain is a rather vague direction, to say the least. Not," he spoke to Ashe now, "that you didn't do all you could, Ashe. And you, McNeil, nothing to add?"

"No, sir. They jumped us out of the blue when Sandy thought he had every possible line tapped, every safeguard working. I don't know how they caught on to us, unless they located our beam to this post. If so, they must have been deliberately hunting us for some time, because we only used the beam as scheduled—"

"The Reds have patience and brains and probably some more of their surprise gadgets to help them. We have the patience and the brains, but not the gadgets.

And time is against us. Get anything out of this, Webb?" Millaird asked the hitherto silent third member of his ruling committee.

The quiet man adjusted his glasses on the bridge of his nose, a flattish nose which did not support them very well. "Just another point to add to our surmises. I would say that they are located somewhere near the Baltic Sea. There are old trade routes there, and in our own time it is a territory closed to us. We never did know too much about that section of Europe. Their installation may be close to the Finnish border. They could disguise their modern station under half a dozen covers; that is a strange country."

Millaird's hands unfolded and he produced a notebook and pen from a shirt pocket. "Won't hurt to stir up some of the present-day agents of the M.I. and the rest. They might just come up with a useful hint. So you'd say the Baltic. But that is a big slice of country."

Webb nodded. "We have one advantage—the old trade routes. In the Beaker period they are pretty well marked. The major one into that section was established for the amber trade. The country is forested, but not so heavily as it was in an earlier period. The native tribes are mostly roving hunters, and fishermen along the coast. But they have had contact with traders." He shoved his glasses back into place with a nervous gesture. "The Reds may run into trouble themselves there at this time—"

"How?" Kelgarries demanded.

"Invasion of the ax people. If they have not yet arrived, they are due very soon. They formed one of the big waves of migratory people, who flooded the country, settled there. Eventually they became the Norse of Celtic stock. We don't know whether they stamped out the native tribes they found there or assimilated them."

"That might be a nice point to have settled more definitely," McNeil commented. "It could mean the difference between getting your skull split and continuing to breathe."

"I don't think they would tangle with the traders. Evidence found today suggests that the Beaker folk simply went on about their business in spite of a change in customers," Webb returned.

"Unless they were pushed into violence." Ashe handed his empty mug to Ross. "Don't forget Lurgha's Wrath. From now on our enemies might take a very dim view of any Beaker trade posts near their property."

Webb shook his head slowly. "A wholesale attack on Beaker establishments would constitute a shift in history. The Reds won't dare that, not just on general suspicion. Remember, they are not any more eager to tinker with history than we are. No, they will watch for us. We will have to stop communication by radio—"

"We can't!" snapped Millaird vehemently. "We can cut it down, but I won't send the boys out without some means of quick communication. You lab boys put your brains to work and see what you can turn out in the way of talk boxes that they can't snoop. Time!" He drummed on his knee with his thick fingers. "It all comes back to a question of time."

"Which we do not have," Ashe observed in his usual quiet voice. "If the Reds are afraid they have been spotted, they must be dismantling their post right now, working around the clock. We'll never again have such a good chance to nail them. We must move now."

Millaird's lids drooped almost shut; he might have

been napping. Kelgarries stirred restlessly by the
door, and Webb's round face had settled into what
looked like permanent lines of disapproval.

"Doc," Millaird spoke over his shoulder to the
fourth man of his following, "what is your report?"

"Ashe must be under treatment for at least five
days. McNeil's burns aren't too bad, and Murdock's
slash is almost healed."

"Five days—" Millaird droned, and then flashed a
glance at the major. "Personnel. We're tied down
without any useful personnel. Who in processing
could be switched without tangling them up entirely?"

"No one. I can recall Jansen and Van Wyke. These
ax people might be a good cover for them." The
momentary light in Kelgarries' eyes faded. "No, we
have no proper briefing and can't get it until the tribe
does appear on the map. I won't send any men in
cold. Their blunders would not only endanger them
but might menace the whole project."

"So that leaves us with you three," Millaird said.
"We'll recall what men we can and brief them again
as fast as possible. But you know how long that will
take. In the meantime—"

Ashe spoke directly to Webb. "You can't pinpoint
the region closer than just the Baltic?"

"We can do this much," the other answered him
slowly, and with obvious reluctance. "We can send
the sub cruising offshore there for the next five days.
If there is any radio activity—any communication—
we should be able to trace the beams. It all depends
upon whether the Reds have any parties operating
from their post. Flimsy—"

"But something!" Kelgarries seized upon it with
the relief of one who needed action.

"And they will be waiting for just such a move on

our part," Webb continued deliberately.

"All right, so they'll be watching!" the major said, about to lose his temper, "but it is about the only move we can make to back up the boys when they do go in."

He whipped around the door and was gone. Webb got up slowly. "I will work over the maps again," he told Ashe. "We haven't scouted that area, and we don't dare send a photoplane over it now. Any trip in will be a stab in the dark."

"When you have only one road, you take it," Ashe replied. "I'll be glad to see anything you can show me, Miles."

If Ross had believed that his pre-trial-run cramming had been a rigorous business, he was soon to laugh at that estimation. Since the burden of the next jump would rest on only three of them—Ashe, McNeil, and himself—they were plunged into a whirlwind of instruction, until Ross, dazed and too tired to sleep on the third night, believed that he was more completely bewildered than indoctrinated. He said as much sourly to McNeil.

"Base has pulled back three other teams," McNeil replied. "But the men have to go to school again, and they won't be ready to come on for maybe three, four weeks. To change runs means unlearning stuff as well as learning it—"

"What about new men?"

"Don't think Kelgarries isn't out now beating the bushes for some! Only, we have to be fitted to the physical type we are supposed to represent. For instance, set a small, dark-headed pugnose among your Norse sea rovers, and he's going to be noticed—maybe remembered too well. We can't afford to take that chance. So Kelgarries had to discover men who not only look the part but are also temperamentally fitted for this job. You can't plant a fellow who thinks as a seaman—not a seaman, you understand, but one whose mind works in that pattern—among a wandering tribe of cattle herders. The protection for the man and the project lies in his being fitted into the right spot at the right time."

Ross had never really thought of that point before. Now he realized that he and Ashe and McNeil were of a common mold. All about the same height, they shared brown hair and light eyes—Ashe's blue, his own gray, and McNeil's hazel—and they were of similar build, small-boned, lean, and quick-moving. He had not seen any of the true Beakermen except on the films. But now, recalling those, he could see that the three time traders were of the same general physical type as the far-roving people they used as a cover.

It was on the morning of the fifth day while the three were studying a map Webb had produced that Kelgarries, followed at his own weighty pace by Millaird, burst in upon them.

"We have it! This time *we* have the luck! The Reds slipped. Oh, how they slipped!"

Webb watched the major, a thin little smile pulling at his pursed mouth. "Miracles sometimes do happen," he remarked. "I suppose the sub has a fix for us."

Kelgarries passed over the flimsy strip of paper he had been waving as a banner of triumph. Webb read the notation on it and bent over the map, making a mark with one of those needle-sharp pencils which seemed to grow in his breast pocket, ready for use. Then he made a second mark.

"Well, it narrows it a bit," he conceded. Ashe looked in turn and laughed.

"I would like to hear your definition of 'narrow' sometime, Miles. Remember we have to cover this on foot, and a difference of twenty miles can mean a lot."

"That mark is quite a bit in from the sea." McNeil offered his own protest when he saw the marking. "We don't know that country—"

Webb shoved his glasses back for the hundredth time that morning. "I suppose we could consider this critical, condition red," he said in such a dubious tone that he might have been begging someone to protest his statement. But no one did. Millaird was busy with the map.

"I think we do, Miles!" He looked to Ashe. "You'll parachute in. The packs with which you will be equipped are special stuff. Once you have them off sprinkle them with a powder Miles will provide and in ten minutes there won't be enough of them left for anyone to identify. We haven't but a dozen of these, and we can't throw them away except in a crisis. Find the base and rig up the detector. Your fix in this time will be easy—but it is the other end of the line we must have. Until you locate that, stick to the job. Don't communicate with us until you have it!"

"There is the possibility," Ashe pointed out, "the Reds may have more than one intermediate post. They probably have played it smart and set up a series of them to spoil a direct trace, as each would lead only to another farther back in time—"

"All right. If that proves true, just get us the next one back," Millaird returned. "From that we can trace them along if we must send in some of the boys wearing dinosaur skins later. We *have* to find their primary base, and if that hunt goes the hard way, well, we do it the hard way."

"How did you get the fix?" McNeil asked.

"One of their field parties ran into trouble and yelled for help."

"Did they get it?"

The major grinned. "What do you think? You know the rules—and the ones the Reds play by are twice as tough on their own men."

"What kind of trouble?" Ashe wanted to know.

"Some kind of a local religious dispute. We do our best with their code, but we're not a hundred percent perfect in reading it, I gather they were playing with a local god and got their fingers burned."

"Lurgha again, eh?" Ashe smiled.

"Foolish," Webb said impatiently. "That is a silly thing to do. You were almost over the edge of prudence yourself, Gordon, with that Lurgha business. To use the Great Mother was a ticklish thing to try, and you were lucky to get out of it so easily."

"Once was enough," Ashe agreed. "Though using it may have saved our lives. But I assure you I am not starting a holy war or setting up as a prophet."

Ross had been taught something of map reading, but mentally he could not make what he saw on paper resemble the countryside. A few landmarks, if there were any outstanding ones, were all he could hope to impress upon his memory until he was actually on the ground.

Landing there according to Millaird's instruction was another experience he would not have chosen of his own accord. To jump was a matter of timing, and in the dark with a measure of rain thrown in, the action was anything but pleasant. Leaving the plane in a blind, follow-the-leader fashion, Ross found the descent into darkness one of the worst trials he had yet faced. But he did not make too bad a landing in the small parklike expanse they had chosen for their target.

Ross pulled loose his harness and chute, dragging them to what he judged to be the center of the clearing. Hearing a plaintive bray from the air, he dodged as one of the two burden asses sent to join them landed and began to kick at its trappings. The animals they had chosen were the most docile available and they had been given sedation before the jump so that now, feeling Ross's hands, the donkey stood quietly while Ross stripped it of its hanging straps.

"Rossa—" The sound of his Beaker name called through the dark brought Ross facing in the other direction.

"Here, and I have one of the donkeys."

"And I the other!" That was McNeil.

Their eyes adjusted to a gloom which was not as thick as it would be in the forest and they worked fast. Then they dragged the parachutes together in a heap. The rain would, Webb had assured them, add to the rapid destruction wrought by the chemical he had provided. Ashe shook it over the pile, and there was a faint greenish glow. Then they moved away to the woodland and made camp for the balance of the night.

So much of their whole exploit depended upon luck, and this small part had been successful. Unless some agent had been stationed to watch for their arrival Ross believed they could not be spotted.

The rest of their plan was elastic. Posing as traders who had come to open a new station, they were to stay near a river which drained a lake and then angled southward to the distant sea. They knew this section was only sparsely settled by small tribes, hardly larger than family clans. These people were generations behind the civilized level of the villagers of Britain—roving hunters who followed the sweep of game north or south with the seasons.

Along the seashore the fishermen had established more permanent holdings which were slowly becoming towns. There were perhaps a few hardy pioneer farmers on the southern fringes of the district, but the principle reason traders came to this region was to get amber and furs. The Beaker people dealt in both.

Now as the three sheltered under the wide branches of a towering pine Ashe fumbled with a pack and brought out the "beaker" which was the identifying mark of his adopted people. He measured into it a portion of the sour, stimulating drink which the traders introduced wherever they went. The cup passed from hand to hand, its taste unpleasant on the tongue, but comfortingly warm to one's middle.

They took turns keeping the watch until the gray of false dawn became the clearer light of morning. After breakfasting on flat cakes of meal, they packed the donkeys, using the same knots and cross lashing which were the mark of real Beaker traders. Their bows protected from dampness under their cloaks, they set out to find the river and their path southward.

Ashe led, Ross towed the donkeys, and McNeil brought up the rear. In the absence of a path they had to set a ragged course, keeping to the edge of the clearing until they saw the end of the lake.

"Woodsmoke," Ashe commented when they had completed two thirds of their journey. Ross sniffed and was able to smell it too. Nodding to Ashe, McNeil oozed into nothingness between the trees with an ease Murdock envied. As they waited for him to return, Ross became conscious of another life about them, one busy with its own concerns, which were in no way those of human beings, except that food and perhaps shelter were to be reckoned among them.

In Britain, Ross had known there were others of his kind about, but this was different. Here, he could have believed it if he had been told he was the first man to walk this way.

A squirrel ran out on a tree limb and surveyed the two men with curious beady eyes, then clung head down on the tree trunk to see them better. One of the donkeys tossed its head, and the squirrel was gone with a flirt of its tail. Although it was quiet, there was a hum underneath the surface which Ross tried to analyze, to identify the many small sounds which went into its making.

Perhaps because he was trying so hard, he noted the faint noise. His hand touched Ashe's arm and a slight movement of his head indicated the direction of the sound. Then, as fluidly as he had melted into the woods, McNeil returned. "Company," he said in a soft voice.

"What kind?"

"Tribesmen, but wilder than any I've seen, even on the tapes. We are certainly out on the fringes now. These people look about cave level. I don't think they've ever heard of traders."

"How many?"

"Three, maybe four families. Most of the males must be out hunting, but there're about ten children and six or seven women. I don't think they've had good luck lately by the look of them."

"Maybe their luck and ours are going to run together," Ashe said, motioning Ross forward with the donkeys. "We will circle about them to the river and then try bartering later. But I do want to establish contact."

9

"Not to be too hopeful—" McNeil rubbed his arm across his hot face—"so far, so good." After kicking from his path some of the branches Ross had lopped from the trees they had been felling, he went to help his companion roll another small log up to a shelter which was no longer temporary. If there had been any eyes other than the woodland hunters' to spy upon them, they would have seen only the usual procedure of the Beaker traders, busily constructing one of their posts.

That they were being watched by the hunters, all three were certain. That there might be other spies in the forest, they had to assume for their own safety. They might prowl at night, but in the daytime all of the time agents kept within the bounds of the roles they were acting.

Barter with the head men of the hunting clan had brought those shy people into the camp of the strangers who had such wonders to exchange for tanned deer hides and better furs. The news of the traders' arrival spread quickly during the short time they had been here, so that two other clans had sent men to watch the proceedings.

With the trade came news which the agents sifted and studied. Each of them had a list of questions to insert into their conversations with the tribesmen if and when that was possible. Although they did not share a common speech with the forest men, signs were informative and certain nouns could be quickly learned. In the meantime Ashe became friendly with the nearest and first of the clan groups they discovered, going hunting with the men as an excuse to penetrate the unknown section they must quarter in their search for the Red base.

Ross drank river water and mopped his own hot face. "If the Reds aren't traders," he mused aloud, "what *is* their cover?"

McNeil shrugged. "A hunting tribe—fishermen—"

"Where would they get the women and children?"

"The same way they get their men—recruit them in our own time. Or in the way lots of tribes grew during periods of stress."

Ross set down the water jug. "You mean, kill off the men, take over their families?" This was a cold-bloodedness he found sickening. Although he had always prided himself on his toughness, several times during his training at the project he had been confronted by things which shook his belief in his own strong stomach and nerve.

"It has been done," McNeil remarked bleakly, "hundreds of times by invaders. In this setup—small family clans, widely scattered—that move would be very easy."

"They would have to pose as farmers, not hunters," Ross pointed out. "They couldn't move a base around with them."

"All right, so they set up a farming village. Oh, I see what you mean—there isn't any village around here. Yet they are here, maybe underground."

How right their guesses were they learned that night when Ashe returned, a deer's haunch on his shoulder. Ross knew him well enough by now to sense his preoccupation. "You found something?"

"A new set of ghosts," Ashe replied with a strange little smile.

"Ghosts!" McNeil pounced upon that. "The Reds like to play the supernatural angle, don't they? First the voice of Lurgha and now ghosts. What do these ghosts do?"

"They inhabit a bit of mountainous territory southeast of here, a stretch taboo for all hunters. We were following a bison track until the beast headed for the ghost country. Then Ulffa called us off in a hurry. It seems that the hunter who goes in there after his quarry never reappears, or if he does, it's in a damaged condition, blown upon by ghosts and burned to death! That's one point."

He sat down by the fire and stretched his arms wearily. "The second is a little more disturbing for us. A Beaker camp about twenty miles south of here, as far as I can judge, was exterminated just a week ago. The message was passed to me because I was thought to be a kinsman of the slain—"

McNeil sat up. "Done because they were hunting us?"

"Might well be. On the other hand, the affair may have been just one of general precaution."

"The ghosts did it?" Ross wanted to know.

"I asked that. No, it seems that strange tribesmen overran it at night."

"At night?" McNeil whistled.

"Just so." Ashe's tone was dry. "The tribes do not

fight that way. Either someone slipped up in his briefing, or the Reds are overconfident and don't care
about the rules. But it was the work of tribesmen, or
their counterfeits. There is also a nasty rumor speed-
ing about that the ghosts do not relish traders and
that they might protest intrusions of such with penal-
ties all around—"

"Like the Wrath of Lurgha," supplied Ross.

"There is a certain repetition in this which suggests
a lot to the suspicious mind," Ashe agreed.

"I'd say no more hunting expeditions for the
present," McNeil said. "It is too easy to mistake a
friend for a deer and weep over his grave afterward."

"That is a thought which entered my mind several
times this afternoon," Ashe agreed. "These people
are deceptively simple on the surface, but their minds
do not work along the same patterns as ours. We try
to outwit them, but it takes only one slip to make it
fatal. In the meantime, I think we'd better make this
place a little more snug, and it might be well to post
sentries as unobtrusively as possible."

"How about faking some signs of a ruined camp
and heading into the blue ourselves?" McNeil asked.
"We could strike for the ghost mountains, traveling
by night, and Ulffa's crowd would think we were finished off."

"An idea to keep in mind. The point against it
would be the missing bodies. It seems that the
tribesmen who raided the Beaker camp left some very
distasteful evidence of what happened to the camp's
personnel. And those we can't produce to cover our
trail."

McNeil was not yet convinced. "We might be able
to fake something along that line, too—"

"We may have to fake nothing," Ross cut in softly.

He was standing close to the edge of the clearing where they were building their hut, his hand on one of the saplings in the palisade they had set up so laboriously that day. Ashe was beside him in an instant.

"What is it?"

Ross's hours of listening to the sounds of the wilderness were his measuring gauge now. "That bird has never called from inland before. It is the blue one we've seen fishing for frogs along the river."

Ashe, not even glancing at the forest, went for the water jug. "Get your trail supplies," he ordered.

Their leather pouches which held enough iron rations to keep them going were always at hand. McNeil gathered them from behind the fur curtain fronting their half-finished cabin. Again the bird called, its cry piercing and covering a long distance. Ross could understand why a careless man would select it for the signal. He crossed the clearing to the donkeys' shelter, slashing through their nose halters. Probably the patient little beasts would swiftly fall victims to some forest prowlers, but at least they would have their chance to escape.

McNeil, his cloak slung about him to conceal the ration bags, picked up the leather bucket as if he were merely going down to the river for water, and came to join Ross. They believed that they were carrying it off well, that the camp must appear normal to any lurkers in the woods. But either they had made some slip or the enemy was impatient. An arrow sped out of the night to flash across the fire, and Ashe escaped death only because he had leaned forward to feed the flames. His arm swung out and sent the water in the jar hissing onto the blaze as he himself rolled in the other direction.

Ross plunged for the brush with McNeil. Lying flat

on the half-frozen ground, they started to work their way to the river bank where the open area would make surprise less possible.

"Ashe?" he whispered and felt McNeil's warm breath on his cheek as he replied:

"He'll make it the other way! He's the best we have for this sort of job."

They made a worm's progress, twice lying, with dagger in hand, while they listened to a faint rustle which betrayed the passing of one of the attackers. Both times Ross was tempted to rise and try to cut off the stranger, but he fought down the impulse. He had learned a control of himself that would have been impossible for him a few months earlier.

The glimmer of the river was pale through the clumps of bushes which sometimes grew into the flood. In this country winter still clung tenaciously in shadowy places with cups of leftover snow, and there was a bite in the wind and water. Ross rose to his knees with an involuntary gasp as a scream cut through the night. He wrenched around toward the camp, only to feel McNeil's hand clamp on his forearm.

"That was a donkey," whispered McNeil urgently. "Come on, let's go down to that ford we discovered!"

They turned south, daring now to trot, half bent to the ground. The river was swollen with spring floods which were only now beginning to subside, but two days earlier they had noticed a sandbar at one spot. By crossing that shelf across the bed, they might hope to put water between them and the unknown enemy tonight. It would give them a breathing space, even though Ross privately shrank from the thought of plowing into the stream. He had seen good-sized trees swirling along in the current only yesterday. And to make such a dash in the dark . . .

From McNeil's throat burst a startling sound which Ross had last heard in Britain—the questing howl of a hunting wolf. The cry was answered seconds later from downstream.

"Ashe!"

They worked their way along the edge of the water with continued care, until they came upon Ashe at last, so much a part of his background that Ross started when the lump he had taken for a bush hunched forward to join them. Together they made the river crossing and turned south again to head for the mountains. It was then that disaster struck.

Ross heard no birdcall warning this time. Though he was on guard, he never sensed the approach of the man who struck him down from behind. One moment he had been trailing McNeil and Ashe; the next moment was black nothingness.

He was aware of a throb of pain which carried throughout his body and then localized in his head. Forcing open his eyes, the dazzle of light was like a spear point striking directly into his head, intensifying his pain to agony. He brought his hand up to his face and felt stickiness there.

"Assha—" He believed he called that aloud, but he did not even hear his own voice. They were in a valley; a wolf had attacked him out of the bushes. Wolf? No, the wolf was dead, but then it came alive again to howl on a river bank.

Ross forced his eyes open once more, enduring the pain of beams he recognized as sunshine. He turned his head to avoid the glare. It was hard to focus, but he fought to steady himself. There was some reason

why it was necessary to move, to get away. But away
from what and where? When Ross tried to think he
could only see muddled pictures which had no con-
nection.

Then a moving object crossed his very narrow field
of vision, passing between him and a thing he knew
was a tree trunk. A four-footed creature with a red
tongue hanging from its jaws. It came toward him
stiff-legged, growling low in its throat, and sniffed at
his body before barking in short excited bursts of
sound.

The noise hurt his head so much that Ross closed
his eyes. Then a shock of icy liquid thrown into his
face aroused him to make a feeble protest and he saw,
hanging over him in a strange upside-down way, a
bearded face which he knew from the past.

Hands were laid on him and the roughness with
which he was moved sent Ross spiraling back into the
dark once again. When he aroused for the second
time it was night and the pain in his head was dulled.
He put out his hands and discovered that he lay on a
pile of fur robes, and was covered by one.

"Assha—" Again he tried that name. But it was not
Assha who came in answer to his feeble call. The
woman who knelt beside him with a horn cup in her
hand had neatly braided hair in which gray strands
showed silver by firelight. Ross knew he had seen her
before, but again where and when eluded him. She
slipped a sturdy arm under his head and raised him
while the world whirled about. The edge of the horn
cup was pressed to his lips, and he drank bitter stuff
which burned in his throat and lit a fire in his insides.
Then he was left to himself once again and in spite of
his pain and bewilderment he slept.

How many days he lay in the camp of Ulffa, tended

by the chief's head wife, Ross found it hard to reckon. It was Frigga who had argued the tribe into caring for a man they believed almost dead when they found him, and who nursed Ross back to life with knowledge acquired through half a hundred exchanges between those wise women who were the doctors and priestesses of these roaming peoples.

Why Frigga had bothered with the injured stranger at all Ross learned when he was able to sit up and marshal his bewildered thoughts into some sort of order. The matriarch of the tribe thirsted for knowledge. That same urge which had led her to certain experiments with herbs, had made her consider Ross a challenge to her healing skill. When she knew that he would live she determined to learn from him all he had to give.

Ulffa and the men of the tribe might have eyed the metal weapons of the traders with awe and avid desire, but Frigga wanted more than trade goods. She wanted the secret of the making of such cloth as the strangers wore, everything she could learn of their lives and the lands through which they had come. She plied Ross with endless questions which he answered as best he could, for he lay in an odd dreamy state where only the present had any reality. The past was dim and far away, and while he was now and then dimly aware that he had something to do, he forgot it easily.

The chief and his men prowled the half-built station after the attackers had withdrawn, bringing back with them a handful of loot—a bronze razor, two skinning knives, some fishhooks, a length of cloth which Frigga appropriated. Ross eyed this spoil indifferently, making no claim upon it. His interest in everything about him was often blanked out by headaches which kept him limp on his bed, uncaring and stupid for hours or even full days.

He gathered that the tribe had been living in fear of an attack from the same raiders who had wiped out the trading post. But at last their scouts returned with the information that the enemy had gone south.

There was one change of which Ross was not aware but which might have startled both Ashe and McNeil. Ross Murdock had indeed died under that blow which had left him unconscious beside the river. The young man whom Frigga had drawn back to sense and a slow recovery was Rossa of the Beaker people. The same Rossa nursed a hot desire for vengeance against those who had struck him down and captured his kinsmen, a feeling which the family tribe who had rescued him could well understand.

There was the same old urgency pushing him to try his strength now, to keep to his feet even when they were unsteady. His bow was gone, but Ross spent hours fashioning another, and he traded his copper bracelet for the best dozen arrows in Ulffa's camp. The jet pin from his cloak he presented to Frigga with all his gratitude.

Now that his strength was coming back he could not rest easy in the camp. He was ready to leave, even though the gashes on his head were still tender to the touch. Ulffa indulgently planned a hunt southward, and Rossa took the trail with the tribesmen.

He broke with the clan hunters when they turned aside at the beginning of the taboo land. Ross, his own mind submerged and taken over by his Beaker cover, hesitated too. Yet he could not give up, and the others left him there, his eyes on the forbidden heights, unhappy and tormented by more than the headaches which still came and went with painful regularity. In the mountains lay what he sought—a hidden something within his brain told him that over and over—but the mountains were taboo, and he should not venture into them.

How long he might have hesitated there if he had not come upon the trail, Ross did not know. But on the day after the hunters of Ulffa's clan left, a glint of sunlight striking between two trees pointed out a woodsman's blaze on a third tree trunk. The two halves of Ross's memory clicked together for an instant as he examined that cut. He knew that it marked a trace and he pushed on, hunting a second cut and then a third. Convinced that these would lead him into the unknown territory, Ross's desire to explore overcame the grafted superstitions of his briefing.

There were other signs that this was an often-traveled route: a spring cleared of leaves and walled with stone, a couple of steps cut in the turf on a steep slope. Ross moved warily, alert to any sound. He might not be an expert woodsman, but he was learning fast, perhaps the faster because his false memories now supplanted the real ones.

That night he built no fire, crawling instead into the heart of a rotted log to sleep, awakening once to the call of a wolf and another time at the distant crash of a dead tree yielding to wind.

In the morning he was about to climb back to the trail he had prudently left the night before when he saw five bearded, fur-clad men looking much the same as Ulffa's people. Ross hugged the earth and watched them pass out of sight before he followed.

All that day he wove up-and-down trail behind the small band, sometimes catching sight of them as they topped a rise well ahead or stopped to eat. It was late afternoon when he crept cautiously to the top of a ridge and gazed down into a valley.

There was a town in that valley, sturdy houses of logs behind a stockade. He had seen towns vaguely like it before, yet it had a dreamlike quality as if it were not as real as it appeared.

Ross rested his chin on his arms and watched that town and the people moving in it. Some were fur-clad hunters, but others dressed quite differently. He started up with a little cry at the sight of one of the men who had walked so swiftly from one house to the next; surely he was a Beaker trader!

His unease grew stronger with every moment he watched, but it was the oddness he sensed in that town which bothered him and not any warning that he, himself, was in danger. He had gotten to his knees to see better when out of nowhere a rope sang through the air, settling about his chest with a vicious jerk which not only drove the air from his lungs but pinioned his arms tight to his body.

10

HAVING BEEN CUFFED and battered into submission more quickly than would have been possible three weeks earlier, Murdock now stood sullenly surveying the man, who, though he dressed like a Beaker trader, persisted in using a language Ross did not know.

"We do not play as children here." At last the man spoke words Ross could understand. "You will answer me or else others shall ask the questions, and less gently. I say to you now—who are you and from where do you come?"

For a moment Ross glowered across the table at him, his inbred antagonism to authority aroused by that contemptuous demand, but then common sense cautioned. His initial introduction to this village had left him bruised and with one of his headaches. There was no reason to let them beat him until he was in no shape to make a break for freedom when and if there was an opportunity.

"I am Rossa of the traders," he returned, eyeing the man with a carefully measured stare. "I came into this land in search of my kinsmen who were taken by raiders in the night."

The man, who sat on a stool by the table, smiled slowly. Again he spoke in the strange tongue, and Ross merely stared stolidly back. His words were short and explosive sounding, and the man's smile faded; his annoyance grew as he continued to speak.

One of Ross's two guards ventured to interrupt, using the Beaker language. "From where did you come?" He was a quiet-faced, slender man, not like his companion, who had roped Murdock from behind and was of the bully breed, able to subdue Ross's wildcat resistance in a very short struggle.

"I came to this land from the south," Ross answered, "after the manner of my people. This is a new land with furs and the golden tears of the sun to be gathered and bartered. The traders move in peace, and their hands are raised against no man. Yet in the darkness there came those who would slay without profit, for what reason I have no knowing."

The quiet man continued the questioning and Ross answered fully with details of the past of one Rossa, a Beaker merchant. Yes, he was from the south. His father was Gurdi, who had a trading post in the warm lands along the big river. This was Rossa's first trip to open new territory. He had come with his father's blood brother, Assha, who was a noted far voyager, and it was an honor to be chosen as donkey-leader for such a one as Assha. With Assha had been Macna, one who was also a far trader, though not as noted as Assha.

Of a certainty, Assha was of his own race! Ross blinked at that question. One need only to look upon him to know that he was of trader blood and no uncivilized woodsrunner. How long had he known Assha? Ross shrugged. Assha had come to his father's post the winter before and had stayed with them through the cold season. Gurdi and Assha had mingled blood after he pulled Gurdi free from the river in flood. Assha had lost his boat and trade goods in that rescue, so Gurdi had made good his loss this year. Detail by detail he gave the story. In spite of the fact that he provided these details glibly, sure that they were true, Ross continued to be haunted by an odd feeling that he was indeed reciting a tale of adventure which had happened long ago and to someone else. Perhaps that pain in his head made him think of these events as very colorless and far away.

"It would seem"—the quiet man turned to the one behind the table—"that this is indeed one Rossa, a Beaker trader."

But the man looked impatient, angry. He made a sign to the other guard, who turned Ross around roughly and sent him toward the door with a shove. Once again the leader gave an order in his own language, adding a few words more with a stinging snap that might have been a threat or a warning.

Ross was thrust into a small room with a hard floor and not even a skin rug to serve as a bed. Since the quiet man had ordered the removal of the ropes from Ross's arms, he leaned against the wall, rubbing the pain of returning circulation away from his wrists and trying to understand what had happened to him and where he was. Having spied upon it from the heights, he knew it wasn't an ordinary trading station, and he wanted to know what they did here. Also, somewhere in this village he hoped to find Assha and Macna.

At the end of the day his captors opened the door only long enough to push inside a bowl and a small jug. He felt for those in the dusk, dipping his fingers into a lukewarm mush of meal and drinking the water from the jug avidly. His headache dulled, and from experience Ross knew that this bout was almost over. If he slept, he would waken with a clearer mind and no pain. Knowing he was very tired, he took the precaution of curling up directly in front of the door so that no one could enter without arousing him.

It was still dark when he awoke with a curious urgency remaining from a dream he could not remember. Ross sat up, flexing his arms and shoulders to combat the stiffness which had come with his cramped sleep. He could not rid himself of a feeling that there was something to be done and that time was his enemy.

Assha! Gratefully he seized on that. He must find Assha and Macna, for the three of them could surely discover a way to get out of this village. That was what was so important!

He had been handled none too gently, and they were holding him a prisoner. But Ross believed that this was not the worst which could happen to him here, and he must be free before the worst did come. The question was, How could he escape? His bow and dagger were gone, and he did not even have his long cloak pin for a weapon, since he had given that to Frigga.

Running his hands over his body, Ross inventoried what remained of his clothing and possessions. He unfastened the bronze chain-belt still buckled in his kilt tunic, swinging the length speculatively in one hand. A masterpiece of craftsmanship, it consisted of patterned plates linked together with a series of five finely wrought chains and a front buckle in the form of a lion's head, its protruding tongue serving as a hook to support a dagger sheath. Its weight promised a weapon of sorts, which when added to the element of surprise might free him.

By rights they would be expecting him to produce some opposition, however. It was well known that only the best fighters, the shrewdest minds, followed the traders' roads. It was a proud thing to be a trader in the wilderness, a thought that warmed Ross now as he waited in the dark for what luck and Ba-Bal of the Bright Horns would send. Were he ever to return to Gurdi's post, Ba-Bal, whose boat rode across the sky from dawn to dusk, would have a fine ox, jars of the first brewing, and sweet-smelling amber laid upon his altar.

Ross had patience which he had learned from the mixed heritage of his two pasts, the real and the false graft. He could wait as he had waited many times before—quiet, and with outward ease—for the right moment to come. It came now with footsteps ringing sharply, halting before his cell door.

With the noiseless speed of a hunting cat, Ross flung himself from behind the door to a wall, where he would be hidden from the newcomer for that necessary instant or two. If his attack was to be successful, it must occur inside the room. He heard the sound of a bar being slid out of its brackets, and he poised himself, the belt rippling from his right hand.

The door was opening inward, and a man stood silhouetted against the outer light. He muttered, looking toward the corner where Ross had thrown his single garment in a roll which might just resemble, for the needed second or two, a man curled in slumber. The man in the doorway took the bait, coming forward far enough for Ross to send the door slamming shut as he himself sprang with the belt aimed for the other's head.

There was a startled cry, cut off in the middle as the belt plates met flesh and bone in a crushing force. Luck was with him! Ross caught up his kilt and belted it around him after he had made a hurried examination of the body now lying at his feet. He was not sure that the man was dead, but at any rate he was completely unconscious. Ross stripped off the man's cloak, located his dagger, freed it from the belt hook and snapped it on his own.

Then inch by inch Ross edged open the door, peering through the crack. As far as he could see, the hall was empty, so he jerked the portal open, and dagger in hand, sprang out, ready for attack. He closed the door, slipping the bar back into its brackets. If the man inside revived and pounded for attention, his own friends might think it was Ross and delay investigating.

But the escape from the cell was the easiest part of what he planned to do, as Ross well knew. To find Assha and Macna in this maze of rooms occupied by the enemy was far more difficult. Although he had no idea in which of the village buildings they might be confined, this one was the largest and seemed to be the headquarters of the chief men, which meant it could also serve as their prison.

Light came from a torch in a bracket halfway down the hall. The wood burned smokily, giving off a resinous odor, and to Ross the glow was sufficient illumination. He slipped along as close to the wall as he could, ready to freeze at the slightest sound. But this portion of the building might well have been deserted, for he saw or heard no one. He tried the only two doors opening out of the hall, but they were secured on the other side. Then he came to a bend in the corridor, and stopped short, hearing a murmur of low voices.

If he had used a hunter's tricks of silent tread and vigilant wariness before, Ross was doubly on guard now as he wriggled to a point from which he could see beyond that turn. Mere luck prevented him from giving himself away a moment later.

Assha! Assha, alive, well, apparently under no restraint, was just turning away from the same quiet man who had had a part in Ross's interrogation. That was surely Assha's brown hair, his familiar tilt of the head convinced Ross, though he could not see the man's face. The quiet man went down the hall, leaving Assha before a door. As he passed through it Ross sped forward and followed him inside.

Assha had crossed the bare room and was standing on a glowing plate in the floor. Ross, aroused to desperate action by some fear he did not understand, leaped after him. His left hand fell upon Assha's shoulder, turning the man half around as Ross, too, stepped upon the patch of luminescence.

Murdock had only an instant to realize that he was staring into the face of an astonished stranger. His hands flashed up in an edgewise blow which caught the other on the side of the throat, and then the world came apart about them. There was a churning, whirling sickness which gripped and bent Ross almost double across the crumpled body of his victim. He held his head lest it be torn from his shoulders by the spinning thing which seemed based behind his eyes.

The sickness endured only for a moment, and some buried part of Ross's mind accepted it as a phenomenon he had experienced before. He came out of it gasping, to focus his attention once more on the man at his feet.

The stranger was still breathing. Ross stooped to drag him from the plate and began binding and gagging him with lengths torn from his kilt. Only when his captive was secure did he begin looking about him curiously.

The room was bare of any furnishings and now, as he glanced at the floor, Ross saw that the plate had lost its glow. The Beaker trader Rossa rubbed sweating palms on his kilt and thought fleetingly of forest ghosts and other mysteries. Not that the traders bowed to those ghosts which were the plague of lesser men and tribes, but anything which suddenly appeared and then disappeared without any logical explanation, needed thinking on. Murdock pulled the prisoner, who was now reviving, to the far end of the room and then went back to the plate with the persistence of a man who refused to treat with ghosts and wanted something concrete to explain the unexplainable. Though he rubbed his hands across the smooth surface of the plate, it did not light up again.

His captive having writhed himself half out of the corner of the room, Ross debated the wisdom of another silencing—say a tap on the skull with the heavy hilt of his dagger. Deciding against it because he might need a guide, he freed the victim's ankle bonds and pulled him to his feet, holding the dagger ready where the man could see it. Were there any more surprises to be encountered in this place, Assha's double would test them first.

The door did not lead to the same corridor, or even the same kind of corridor Ross had passed through moments earlier. Instead they entered a short passage with walls of some smooth stuff which had almost the sheen of polished metal and were sleek and cold to the touch. In fact, the whole place was chill, chill as river water in the spring.

Still herding the prisoner before him, Ross came to the nearest door and looked within, to be faced by

incomprehensible frames of metal rods and boxes.
Rossa of the traders marveled and stared, but again,
he realized that what he saw was not altogether
strange. Part of one wall was a board on which small
lights flashed and died, to flash again in winks of
bright color. A mysterious object made of wire and
disks hung across the back of a chair standing near-
by.

The bound man lurched for the chair and fell, rolling
toward the wall. Ross pushed him on until he was
hidden behind one of the metal boxes. Then he made
the rounds of the room, touching nothing, but studying what he could not understand. Puffs of warm air
came in through grills near the floor, but the room
had the same general chill as the hall outside.

Meanwhile the lights on the board had become
more active, flashing on and off in complex patterns.
Ross now heard a buzzing, as if a swarm of angry
insects were gathered for an attack. Crouching beside
his captive, Ross watched the lights, trying to discover the source of the sound.

The buzz grew shriller, almost demanding. Ross
heard the tramp of heavy footgear in the corridor,
and a man entered the room, crossing purposefully to
the chair. He sat down and drew the wire-and-disk
frame over his head. His hands moved under the
lights, but Ross could not guess what he was doing.

The captive at Murdock's side tried to stir, but
Ross's hand pinned him quiet. The shrill noise which
had originally summoned the man at the lights was
interrupted by a sharp pattern of long-and-short
sounds, and his hands flew even more quickly while
Ross took in every detail of the other's clothing and
equipment. He was neither a shaggy tribesman nor a
trader. He wore a dull-green outer garment cut in one

piece to cover his arms and legs as well as his body, and his hair was so short that his round skull might have been shaven. Ross rubbed the back of his wrist across his eyes, experiencing again that dim other memory. Odd as this man looked, Murdock had seen his like before somewhere, yet the background had not been Gurdi's post on the southern river. Where and when had he, Rossa, ever been with such strange beings? And why could he not remember it all more clearly?

Boots sounded once more in the hall, and another figure strode in. This one wore furs, but he, too, was no woods hunter, Ross realized as he studied the newcomer in detail. The loose overshirt of thick fur with its hood thrown back, the high boots, and all the rest were not of any primitive fashioning. And the man had four eyes! One pair were placed normally on either side of his nose, and the other two, black-rimmed and murky, were set above on his forehead.

The fur-clad man tapped the one seated at the board. He freed his head partially from the wire cage so that they could talk together in a strange language while lights continued to flash and the buzzing died away. Ross's captive wriggled with renewed vigor and at last thrashed free a foot to kick at one of the metal installations. The resulting clang brought both men around. The one at the board tore his head cage off as he jumped to his feet, while the other brought out a gun.

Gun? One little fraction of Ross's mind wondered at his recognition of that black thing and of the danger it promised, even as he prepared for battle. He pushed his captive across the path of the man in fur and threw himself in the other direction. There was a blast to make a torment in his head as he hurled toward the door.

So intent was Ross upon escape that he did not glance behind but skidded out on his hands and knees, thus fortunately presenting a poor target to the third man coming down the hall. Ross's shoulder hit the newcomer at thigh level, and they tangled in a struggling mass which saved Ross's life as the others burst out behind them.

Ross fought grimly, his hands and feet moving in blows he was not conscious of planning. His opponent was no easy match and at last Ross was flattened, in spite of his desperate efforts. He was whirled over, his arms jerked behind him, and cold metal rings snapped about his wrists. Then he was rolled back, to lie blinking up at his enemies.

All three men gathered over him, barking questions which he could not understand. One of them disappeared and returned with Ross's former captive, his mouth a straight line and a light in his eyes Ross understood far better than words.

"You are the trader prisoner?" The man who looked like Assha leaned over Murdock, patches of red on his tanned skin where the gag and wrist bonds had been.

"I am Rossa, son of Gurdi, of the traders," Ross returned, meeting what he read in the other's expression with a ready defiance. "I was a prisoner, yes. But you did not keep me one for long then, nor shall you now."

The man's thin upper lip lifted. "You have done yourself ill, my young friend. We have a better prison here for you, one from which you shall not escape."

He spoke to the other men, and there was the ring of an order in his voice. They pulled Ross to his feet, pushing him ahead of them. During the short march Ross used his eyes, noticing things he could not identify in the rooms through which they passed. Men called questions and at last they paused long enough, Ross firmly in the hold of the fur-clad guard, for the other two to put on similar garments.

Ross had lost his cloak in the fight, but no fur shirt was given him. He shivered more and more as the chill which clung to that warren of rooms and halls bit into his half-clad body. He was certain of only one thing about this place; he could not possibly be in the crude buildings of the valley village. However, he was unable to guess where he was and how he had come there.

Finally, they went down a narrow room filled with bulky metal objects of bright scarlet or violet that gleamed weirdly and were equipped with rods along which all the colors of the rainbow were ringed. Here was a round door, and when one of the guards used both hands to tug it open, the cold that swept in at them was a frigid breath that burned as it touched bare skin.

11

I<small>T TOOK</small> Ross a while to learn that the dirty-white walls of this tunnel which were almost entirely opaque, with dark objects showing dimly through them here and there, were of solid ice. A black wire was hooked overhead and at regular intervals hung with lights which did nothing to break the sensation of glacial cold about them.

Ross shuddered. Every breath he drew stung in his lungs; his bare shoulders and arms and the exposed section of thigh between kilt and boot were numb. He could only move on stiffly, pushed ahead by his guards when he faltered. He guessed that were he to lose his footing here and surrender to the cold, he would forfeit the battle entirely and with it his life.

He had no way of measuring the length of the boring through the solid ice, but they were at last fronted by another opening, a ragged one which might have been hacked with an ax. They emerged from it into the wildest scene Ross had ever seen. Of course, he was familiar with ice and snow, but here was a world surrendered completely to the brutal force of winter in a strange, abnormal way. It was a still, dead white-gray world in which nothing moved save the wind which curled the drifts.

His guards covered their eyes with the murky lenses they had worn pushed up on their foreheads within the shelter, for above them sunlight dazzled on the ice crest. Ross, his eyes smarting, kept his gaze centered on his feet. He was given no time to look about. A rope was produced, a loop of it flipped in a noose about his throat, and he was towed along like a leashed dog. Before them was a path worn in the snow, not only by the passing of booted feet, but with more deeply scored marks as if heavy objects had been sledded there. Ross slipped and stumbled in the ruts, fearing to fall lest he be dragged. The numbness of his body reached into his head, he was dizzy, the world about him misting over now and again with a haze which arose from the long stretches of unbroken snow fields.

Tripping in a rut, he went down upon one knee, his flesh too numbed now to feel the additional cold of the snow, snow so hard that its crust delivered a knife's cut. Unemotionally, he watched a thin line of red trickle in a sluggish drop or two down the blue skin of his leg. The rope jerked him forward, and Ross scrambled awkwardly until one of his captors hooked a fur mitten in his belt and heaved him to his feet once more.

The purpose of that trek through the snow was obscure to Ross. In fact, he no longer cared, save that a hard rebel core deep inside him would not let him give up as long as his legs could move and he had a scrap of conscious will left in him. It was more difficult to walk now. He skidded and went down twice more.

Then, the last time he slipped, he sledded past the man who led him, sliding down the slope of a glass-slick slope. He lay at the foot, unable to get up. Through the haze and deadening blanket of the cold he knew that he was being pulled about, shaken, generally mishandled; but this time he could not respond. Someone snapped open the rings about his wrists.

There was a call, echoing eerily across the ice. The fumbling about his body changed to a tugging and once more he was sent rolling down the slope. But the rope was now gone from his throat, and his arms were free. This time when he brought up hard against an obstruction he was not followed.

Ross's conscious mind—that portion of him that was Rossa, the trader—was content to lie there, to yield to the lethargy born of the frigid world about him. But the subconscious Ross Murdock of the Project prodded at him. He had always had a certain cold hatred which could crystalize and become a spur. Once it had been hatred of circumstances and authority; now it became hatred for those who had led him into this wilderness with the purpose, as he knew now, of leaving him to freeze and die.

Ross pulled his hands under him. Though there was no feeling in them, they obeyed his will clumsily. He levered himself up and looked around. He lay in a narrow crevicelike cut, partly walled in by earth so frozen as to resemble steel. Crusted over it in long streaks from above were tongues of ice. To remain here was to serve his captors' purpose.

Ross inched his way to his feet. This opening, which was intended as his grave, was not so deep as the men had thought it in their hurry to be rid of him. He believed that he could climb out if he could make his body answer to his determination.

Somehow Ross made that supreme effort and came again to the rutted path from which they had tumbled him. Even if he could, there was no sense in going along that rutted trail, for it led back to the ice-encased building from which he had been brought. They had thrust him out to die; they would not take him in.

But a road so well marked must have some goal, and in hopes that he might find shelter at the other end, Ross turned to the left. The trace continued down the slope. Now the towering walls of ice and snow were broken by rocky teeth as if they had bitten deep upon this land, only to be gnawed in return. Rouding one of those rock fangs, Ross looked at a stretch of level ground. Snow lay here, but the beaten-down trail led straight through it to the rounded side of a huge globe half buried in the ground, a globe of dark material which could only be man-made.

Ross was past caution. He must get to warmth and shelter or he was done for, and he knew it. Wavering and weaving, he went on, his attention fixed on the door ahead—a closed oval door. With a sob of exhausted effort, Ross threw himself against it. The barrier gave, letting him fall forward into a queer glimmering radiance of bluish light.

The light rousing him because it promised more, he crawled on past another door which was flattened back against the inner wall. It was like making one's way down a tube. Ross paused, pressing his lifeless hands against his bare chest under the edge of his tunic, suddenly realizing that there was warmth here. His breath did not puff out in frosty streamers before him, nor did the air sear his lungs when he ventured to draw in more than shallow gulps.

With that realization a measure of animal caution

returned to him. To remain where he was, just inside the entrance, was to court disaster. He must find a hiding place before he collapsed, for he sensed he was very near the end of his ability to struggle. Hope had given him a flash of false strength, the impetus to move, and he must make the most of that gift.

His path ended at a wide ladder, coiling in slow curves into gloom below and shadows above. He sensed that he was in a building of some size. He was afraid to go down, for even looking in that direction almost finished his sense of balance, so he climbed up.

Step by step, Ross made that painful journey, passing levels from which three or four hallways ran out like the radii of a spider's web. He was close to the end of his endurance when he heard a sound, echoed, magnified, from below. It was someone moving. He dragged his body into the fourth level where the light was very faint, hoping to crawl far enough into one of the passages to remain unseen from the stair. But he had gone only part-way down his chosen road when he collapsed, panting, and fell back against the wall. His hands pawed vainly against that sleek surface. He was falling through it!

Ross had a second, perhaps two, of stupefied wonder. Lying on a soft surface, he was enfolded by a warmth which eased his bruised and frozen body. There was a sharp prick in his thigh, another in his arm, and the world was a hazy dream until he finally slept in the depths of exhaustion.

There were dreams, detailed ones, and Ross stirred uneasily as his sleep thinned to waking. He lay with his eyes closed, fitting together odd bits of—dreams? No, he was certain that they were memories. Rossa of the Beaker traders and Ross Murdock of the project were again fused into one and the same person. How it had happened he did not know, but it was true.

Opening his eyes, he noticed a curved ceiling of soft blue which misted at the edges into gray. The restful color acted on his troubled, waking mind like a soothing word. For the first time since he had been struck down in the night his headache was gone. He raised his hand to explore that old hurt near his hairline that had been so tender only yesterday that it could not bear pressure. There remained only a thin, rough line like a long-healed scar, that was all.

Ross lifted his head to look about him. His body lay supported in a cradlelike arrangement of metal, almost entirely immersed in a red gelatinous substance with a clean, aromatic odor. Just as he was no longer cold, neither was he hungry. He felt as fit as he ever had in his life. Sitting up in the cradle, he stroked the jelly away from his shoulders and chest. It fell from him cleanly, leaving no trace of grease or dampness on his skin.

There were other fixtures in the small cylinderlike chamber besides that odd bed in which he had lain. Two bucketshaped seats were placed at the narrow fore part of the room and before those seats was a system of controls he could not comprehend.

As Ross swung his feet to the floor there was a click from the side which brought him around, ready for trouble. But the noise had been caused by the opening of a door into a small cupboard. Inside the cupboard lay a fat package. Obviously this was an invitation to investigate the offering.

The package contained a much folded article of fabric, compressed and sealed in a transparent bag which he fumbled twice before he succeeded in releasing its fastening. Ross shook out a garment of material such as he had never seen before. Its sheen and satin-smooth surface suggested metal, but its stuff was as supple as fine silk. Color rippled across it with every twist and turn he gave to the length—dark blue fading to pale violet, accented with wavering streaks of vivid and startling green.

Ross experimented with a row of small, brilliant-green studs which made a transverse line from the right shoulder to the left hip, and they came apart. As he climbed into the suit the stuff modeled to his body in a tight but perfect fit. Across the shoulders were bands of green to match the studs, and the stockinglike tights were soled with a thick substance which formed a cushion for his feet.

He pressed the studs together, felt them lock, and then stood smoothing that strange, beautiful fabric, unable to account for either it or his surroundings. His head was clear; he could remember every detail of his flight up to the time he had fallen through the wall. And he was certain that he had passed through not only one, but two, of the Red time posts. Could this be the third? If so, was he still a captive? Why would they leave him to freeze in the open country one moment and then treat him this way later?

He could not connect the ice-encased building from which the Reds had taken him with this one. At the sound of another soft noise Ross glanced over his shoulder just in time to see the cradle of jelly, from which he had emerged, close in upon itself until its bulk was a third of its former size. Compact as a box, it folded up against the wall.

Ross, his cushioned feet making no sound, advanced to the bucket-chairs. But lowering his body into one of them for a better look at what vaguely resembled the control of a helicopter—like the one in which he had taken the first stage of his fantastic journey across space and time—he did not find it comfortable. He realized that it had not been constructed to accommodate a body shaped precisely like his own.

A body like his own . . . That jelly bath or bed or whatever it was . . . The clothing which adapted so skillfully to his measurements . . .

Ross leaned forward to study the devices on the control board, confirming his suspicions. He had made the final jump of them all! He was now in some building of that alien race upon whose existence Millaird and Kelgarries had staked the entire project. This was the source, or one of the sources, from which the Reds were getting the knowledge which fitted no modern pattern.

A world encased in ice and a building with strange machinery. This thing—a cylinder with a pilot's seat and a set of controls. Was it an alien place? But the jelly bath—and the rest of it . . . Had his presence activated that cupboard to supply him with clothing? And what had become of the tunic he was wearing when he entered?

Ross got up to search the chamber. The bed-bath was folded against the wall, but there was no sign of his Beaker clothing, his belt, the hide boots. He could not understand his own state of well being, the lack of hunger and thirst.

There were two possible explanations for it all. One was that the aliens still lived here and for some reason had come to his aid. The other was that he stood in a place where robot machinery worked, though those who had set it up were no longer there. It was difficult to separate his memory of the half-buried globe he had seen from his sickness of that moment. Yet he knew that he had climbed and crawled through emptiness, neither seeing nor hearing any other life. Now Ross restlessly paced up and down, seeking the door through which he must have come, but there was not even a line to betray such an opening.

"I want out," he said aloud, standing in the center of the cramped room, his fists planted on his hips, his eyes still searching for the vanished door. He had tapped, he had pushed, he had tried every possible way to find it. If he could only remember how he had come in! But all he could recall was leaning against a wall which moved inward and allowed him to fall. But where had he fallen? Into that jelly bath?

Ross, stung by a sudden idea, glanced at the ceiling. It was low enough so that by standing on tiptoes he could drum his fingers on its surface. Now he moved to the place directly above where the cradle had swung before it had folded itself away.

Rapping and poking, his efforts were rewarded at last. The blue curve gave under his assault. He pushed now, rising on his toes, though in that position he could exert little pressure. Then as if some faulty catch had been released, the ceiling swung up so that he lost his footing and would have fallen had he not caught the back of one of the bucket-seats.

He jumped and by hooking his hands over the edge of the opening, was able to work his way up and out, to face a small line of light. His fingers worked at that, and he opened a second door, entering a familiar corridor.

Holding the door open, Ross looked back, his eyes widening at what he saw. For it was plain now that he had just climbed out of a machine with the unmistakable outline of a snub-nosed rocket. The small flyer—or a jet, or whatever it was—had been fitted into a pocket in the side of the big structure as a ship into a berth, and it must have been set there to shoot from that enclosing chamber as a bullet is shot from a rifle barrel. But why?

Ross's imagination jumped from fact to theory. The torpedo craft could be an atomic jet. All right, he had been in bad shape when he fell into it by chance and the bed machine had caught him as if it had been created for just such a duty. What kind of a small plane would be equipped with a restorative apparatus? Only one intended to handle emergencies, to transport badly injured living things who had to leave the building in a hurry.

In other words, a lifeboat!

But why would a building need a lifeboat? That would be rather standard equipment for a ship. Ross stepped into the corridor and stared about him with open and incredulous wonder. Could this be some form of ship, grounded here, deserted and derelict, and now being plundered by the Reds? The facts fitted! They fitted so well with all he had been able to discover that Ross was sure it was true. But he determined to prove it beyond all doubt.

He closed the door leading to the lifeboat berth, but not so securely that he could not open it again. That was too good a hiding place. On his cushioned feet he padded back to the stairway, and he stood there listening. Far below were sounds, a rasp of metal against metal, a low murmur of muted voices. But from above there was nothing, so he would explore above before he ventured into that other danger zone.

Ross climbed, passing two more levels, to come out into a vast room with a curving roof which must fill the whole crown of the globe. Here was such a wealth of machines, controls, things he could not understand that he stood bewildered, content for the moment merely to look. There were—he counted slowly—five control boards like those he had seen in the small escape ship. Each of these was faced by two or three of the bucket-seats, only these swung in webbing. He put his hand on one, and it bobbed elastically.

The control boards were so complicated that the one in the lifeboat might have been a child's toy in comparison. The air in the ship had been good; in the lifeboat it had held the pleasant odor of the jelly; but here Ross sniffed a faint but persistent hint of corruption, of an old malodor.

He left the vantage point by the stairs and paced between the control boards and their empty swinging seats. This was the main control room, of that he was certain. From this point all the vast bulk beneath him had been set in motion, sailed here and there. Had it been on the sea, or through the air? The globe shape suggested an air-borne craft. But a civilization so advanced as this would surely have left some remains. Ross was willing to believe that he could be much farther back in time than 2000 B.C., but he was still sure that traces of those who could build a thing like this would have existed in the twentieth century A.D.

Maybe that was how the Reds had found this. Something they had turned up within their country— say, in Siberia, or some of the forgotten corners of Asia—had been a clue.

Having had little schooling other than the intensive cramming at the base and his own informal education, the idea of the race who had created this ship overawed Ross more than he would admit. If the project could find this, turn loose on it the guys who knew about such things . . . But that was just what they were striving for, and he was the only project man to have found the prize. Somehow, someway, he had to get back—out of this half-buried ship and its icebound world—back to where he could find his own people. Perhaps the job was impossible, but he had to try. His survival was considered impossible by the men who had thrown him into the service, but here he was. Thanks to the men who had built this ship, he was alive and well.

Ross sat down in one of the uncomfortable seats to think and thus avoided immediate disaster, for he was hidden from the stairs on which sounded the tap of boots. A climber, maybe two, were on their way up, and there was no other exit from the control cabin.

12

ROSS DROPPED from the web-slung chair to the floor and made himself as small as possible under the platform at the front of the cabin. Here, where there was a smaller control board and two seats placed closely together, the odd, unpleasant odor clung and became stronger to Ross's senses as he waited tensely for the climbers to appear. Though he had searched, there was nothing in sight even faintly resembling a weapon. In a last desperate bid for freedom he crept back to the stairwell.

He had been taught a blow during his training period, one which required a precise delivery and, he had been warned, was often fatal. He would use it now. The climber was very close. A cropped head arose through the floor opening, and Ross struck, knowing as his hand chopped against the folds of a fur hood that he had failed.

But the impetus of that unexpected blow saved him after all. With a choked cry the man disappeared, crashing down upon the one following him. A scream and shouts were heard from below, and a shot ripped up the well as Ross scrambled away from it. He might have delayed the final battle, but they had him cornered. He faced that fact bleakly. They need only sit below and let nature take its course. His session in the lifeboat had restored his strength, but a man could not live forever without food and water.

However, he had bought himself perhaps a yard of time which must be put to work. Turning to examine the seats, Ross discovered that they could be unhooked from their webbing swings. Freeing all of them, he dragged their weight to the stairwell and jammed them together to make a barricade. It could not hold long against any determined push from below, but, he hoped, it would deflect bullets if some sharp-shooter tried to wing him by ricochet. Every so often there was the crash of a shot and some shouting, but Ross was not going to be drawn out of cover by that.

He paced around the control cabin, still hunting for a weapon. The symbols on the levers and buttons were meaningless to him. They made him feel frustrated because he imagined that among that countless array were some that might help him out of the trap if he could only guess their use.

Once more he stood by the platform thinking. This was the point from which the ship had been sailed— in the air or on some now frozen sea. These control boards must have given the ship's master the means not only of propelling the vast bulk, but of unloading and loading cargo, lighting, heating, ventilation, and perhaps defense! Of course, every control might be dead now, but he remembered that in the lifeboat the machines had worked successfully, fulfilled expertly the duty for which they had been constructed.

The only step remaining was to try his luck. Having made his decision, Ross simply shut his eyes as he had in a very short and almost forgotten childhood, turned around three times, and pointed. Then he looked to see where luck had directed him.

His finger indicated a board before which there had been three seats, and he crossed to it slowly, with a sense that once he touched the controls he might inaugurate a chain of events he could not stop. The crash of a shot underlined the fact that he had no other recourse.

Since the symbols meant nothing. Ross concentrated on the shapes of the various devices and chose one which vaguely resembled the type of light switch he had always known. Since it was up, he pressed it down, counting to twenty slowly as he waited for a reaction. Below the switch was an oval button marked with two wiggles and a double dot in red. Ross snapped it level with the panel, and when it did not snap back, he felt somehow encouraged. When the two levers flanking that button did not push in or move up and down, Ross pulled them out without even waiting to count off.

This time he had results! A cracking of noise with a singsong rhythm, the volume of which, low at first, arose to a drone filled the cabin. Ross, deafened by the din, twisted first one lever and then the other until he had brought the sound to a less piercing howl. But he needed action, not just noise; he moved from behind the first chair to the next one. Here were five oval buttons, marked in the same vivid green as that which trimmed his clothing—two wiggles, a dot, a double bar, a pair of entwined circles, and a crosshatch.

Why make a choice? Recklessness bubbled to the

surface, and Ross pushed all the buttons in rapid succession. The results were, in a measure, spectacular. Out of the top of the control board rose a triangle of screen which steadied and stood firm while across it played a rippling wave of color. Meanwhile the singsong became an angry squawking as if in protest.

Well, he had something, even if he didn't know what it was! And he had also proved that the ship was alive. However, Ross wanted more than a squawk of exasperation, which was exactly what the noise had become. It almost sounded, Ross decided as he listened, as if he were being expertly chewed out in another language. Yes, he wanted more than a series of squawks and a fanciful display of light waves on a screen.

At the section of board before the third and last seat there was less choice—only two switches. As Ross flicked up the first, the pattern on the screen dwindled into a brown color shot with cream in which there was a suggestion of a picture. Suppose one didn't put the switch all the way up? Ross examined the slot in which the bar moved and now noted a series of tiny point marks along it. Selective? It would not do any harm to see. First he hurried back to the cork of chairs he had jammed into the stairwell. The squawks were now coming only at intervals, and Ross could hear nothing to suggest that his barrier was being forced.

He returned to the lever and moved it back two notches, standing open-mouthed at the immediate result. The cream-and-brown streaks were making a picture! Moving another notch down caused the picture to skitter back and forth on the screen. With memories of TV tuning to guide him, Ross brought the other lever down to a matching position, and the dim and shadowy images leaped into clear and complete focus. But the color was still brown, not the black and white he had expected.

Only, he was also looking into a face! Ross swallowed, his hand grasping one of the strings of chair webbing for support. Perhaps because in some ways it did resemble his own, that face was more preposterously nonhuman. The visage on the screen was sharply triangular with a small, sharply pointed chin and a jaw line running at an angle from a broad upper face. The skin was dark, covered largely with a soft and silky down, out of which hooked a curved and shining nose set between two large round eyes. On top of that astonishing head the down rose to a peak not unlike a cockatoo's crest. Yet there was no mistaking the intelligence in those eyes, nor the other's amazement at sight of Ross. They might have been staring at each other through a window.

Squawk . . . squeek . . . squawk . . . The creature in the mirror—on the vision plate—or outside the window—moved its absurdly small mouth in time to those sounds. Ross swallowed again and automatically made answer.

"Hello." His voice was a weak whistle, and perhaps it did not reach the furry-faced one, for he continued his questions if questions they were. Meanwhile Ross, over his first stupefaction, tried to see something of the creature's background. Though the objects were slightly out of focus, he was sure he recognized fittings similar to those about him. He must be in communication with another ship of the same type and one which was not deserted!

Furry-face had turned his head away to squawk rapidly over his shoulder, a shoulder which was crossed by a belt or sash with an elaborate pattern.

Then he got up from his seat and stood aside to make room for the one he had summoned.

If Furry-face had been a startling surprise, Ross was now to have another. The man who now faced him on the screen was totally different. His skin registered as pale—cream-colored—and his face was far more human in shape, though it was hairless as was the smooth dome of his skull. When one became accustomed to that egg slickness, the stranger was not bad-looking, and he was wearing a suit which matched the one Ross had taken from the lifeboat.

This one did not attempt to say anything. Instead, he stared at Ross long and measuringly, his eyes growing colder and less friendly with every second of that examination. Ross had resented Kelgarries back at the project, but the major could not match Baldy for the sheer weight of unpleasant warning he could pack into a look. Ross might have been startled by Furry-face, but now his stubborn streak arose to meet this implied challenge. He found himself breathing hard and glaring back with an intensity which he hoped would get across and prove to Baldy that he would not have everything his own way if he proposed to tangle with Ross.

His preoccupation with the stranger on the screen betrayed Ross into the hands of those from below. He heard their attack on the barricade too late. By the time he turned around, the cork of seats was heaved up and a gun was pointing at his middle. His hands went up in small reluctant jerks as that threat held him where he was. Two of the fur-clad Reds climbed into the control chamber.

Ross recognized the leader as Ashe's double, the man he had followed across time. He blinked for just an instant as he faced Ross and then shouted an order at his companion. The other spun Murdock around, bringing his hands down behind him to clamp his wrists together. Once again Ross fronted the screen and saw Baldy watching the whole scene with an expression suggesting that he had been shocked out of his complacent superiority.

"Ah . . ." Ross's captors were staring at the screen and the unearthly man there. Then one flung himself at the control panel and his hands whipped back and forth, restoring to utter silence both screen and room.

"What are you?" The man who might have been Ashe spoke slowly in the Beaker tongue, drilling Ross with his stare as if by the force of his will alone he could pull the truth out of his prisoner.

"What do you think I am?" Ross countered. He was wearing the uniform of Baldy, and he had clearly established contact with the time owners of this ship. Let that worry the Red!

But they did not try to answer him. At a signal he was led to the stair. To descend that ladder with his hands behind him was almost impossible, and they had to pause at the next level to unclasp the handcuffs and let him go free. Keeping a gun on him carefully, they hurried along, trying to push the pace while Ross delayed all he could. He realized that in his recognition of the power of the gun back in the control chamber, his surrender to its threat, he had betrayed his real origin. So he must continue to confuse the trail to the project in every possible way left to him. He was sure that this time they would not leave him in the first convenient crevice.

He knew he was right when they covered him with a fur parka at the entrance to the ship, once more manacling his hands and dropping a noose leash on him.

So, they were taking him back to their post here. Well, in the post was the time transporter which could return him to his own kind. It would be, it must be possible to get to that! He gave his captors no more trouble but trudged, outwardly dispirited, along the rutted way through the snow up the slope and out of the valley.

He did manage to catch a good look at the globe-ship. More than half of it, he judged, was below the surface of the ground. To be so buried it must either have lain there a long time or, if it were an air vessel, crashed hard enough to dig itself that partial grave. Yet Ross had established contact with another ship like it, and neither of the creatures he had seen were human, at least not human in any way he knew.

Ross chewed on that as he walked. He believed that those with him were looting the ship of its cargo, and by its size, that cargo must be a large one. But cargo from where? Made by what hands, what *kind* of hands? Enroute to what port? And how had the Reds located the ship in the first place? There were plenty of questions and very few answers. Ross clung to the hope that somehow he had endangered the Reds' job here by activating the communication system of the derelict and calling the attention of its probable owners to its fate.

He also believed that the owners might take steps to regain their property. Baldy had impressed him deeply during those few moments of silent appraisal, and he knew he would not like to be on the receiving end of any retaliation from the other. Well, now he had only one chance, to keep the Reds guessing as long as he could and hope for some turn of fate which would allow him to try for the time transport. How the plate operated he did not know, but he had been transferred here from the Beaker age and if he could return to that time, escape might be possible. He had only to reach the river and follow it down to the sea where the sub was to make rendezvous at intervals. The odds were overwhelmingly against him, and Ross knew it. But there was no reason, he decided, to lie down and roll over dead to please the Reds.

As they approached the post Ross realized how much skill had gone into its construction. It looked as if they were merely coming up to the outer edge of a glacier tongue. Had it not been for the track in the snow, there would have been no reason to suspect that the ice covered anything but a thick core of its own substance. Ross was shoved through the white-walled tunnel to the building beyond.

He was hurried through the chain of rooms to a door and thrust through, his hands still fastened. It was dark in the cubby and colder than it had been outside. Ross stood still, waiting for his eyes to adjust to the gloom. It was several moments after the door had slammed shut that he caught a faint thud, a dull and hollow sound.

"Who is here?" he used the Beaker speech, determining to keep to the rags of his cover, which probably was a cover no longer. There was no reply, but after a pause that distant beat began again. Ross stepped cautiously forward, and by the simple method of running fullface into the walls, discovered that he was in a bare cell. He also discovered that the noise lay behind the left-hand wall, and he stood with his ear flat against it, listening. The sound did not have the regular rhythm of a machine in use—there were odd pauses between some blows, others came in a quick rain. It was as if someone were digging!

Were the Reds engaged in enlarging their icebound headquarters? Having listened for a considerable time, Ross doubted that, for the sound was too irregular. It seemed almost as if the longer pauses were used to check up on the result of labor—was it the extent of the excavation or the continued preservation of secrecy?

Ross slipped down along the wall, his shoulders still resting against it, and rested with his head twisted so he could hear the tapping. Meanwhile he flexed his wrists inside the hoops which confined them, and folding his hands as small as possible, tried to slip them through the rings. The only result was that he chafed his skin raw to no advantage. They had not taken off his parka, and in spite of the chill about him, he was too warm. Only that part of his body covered by the suit he had taken from the ship was comfortable; he could almost believe that it possessed some built-in conditioning device.

With no hope of relief Ross rubbed his hands back and forth against the wall, scraping the hoops on his wrists. The distant pounding had ceased, and this time the pause lengthened into so long a period that Ross fell asleep, his head falling forward on his chest, his raw wrists still pushed against the surface behind him.

He was hungry when he awoke, and with that hunger his rebellion sparked into flame. Awkwardly he got to his feet and lurched along to the door through which he had been thrown, where he proceeded to kick at the barrier. The cushiony stuff forming the soles of his tights muffled most of the force of those blows, but some noise was heard outside, for the door opened and Ross faced one of the guards.

"Food! I want to eat!" He put into the Beaker language all the resentment boiling in him.

The fellow ignoring him, reached in a long arm, and nearly tossing the prisoner off balance, dragged him out of the cell. Ross was marched into another room to face what appeared to be a tribunal. Two of the men there he knew—Ashe's double and the quiet man who had questioned him back in the other time station. The third, clearly one of greater authority, regarded Ross bleakly.

"Who are you?" the quiet man asked.

"Rossa, son of Gurdi. And I would eat before I make talk with you. I have not done any wrong that you should treat me as a barbarian who has stolen salt from the trading post—"

"You are an agent," the leader corrected him dispassionately, "of whom you will tell us in due time. But first you shall speak of the ship, of what you found there, and why you meddled with the controls . . . Wait a moment before you refuse, my young friend." He raised his hand from his lap, and once again Ross faced an automatic. "Ah, I see that you know what I hold—odd knowledge for an innocent Bronze Age trader. And please have no doubts about my hesitation to use this. I shall not kill you, naturally," the man continued, "but there are certain wounds which supply a maximum of pain and little serious damage. Remove his parka, Kirschov."

Once more Ross was unmanacled, the fur stripped from him. His questioner carefully studied the suit he wore under it. "Now you will tell us exactly what we wish to hear."

There was a confidence in that statement which chilled Ross; Major Kelgarries had displayed its like. Ashe had it in another degree, and certainly it had been present in Baldy. There was no doubt that the speaker meant exactly what he said. He had at his command methods which would wring from his captive the full sum of what he wanted, and there would be no consideration for that captive during the process.

His implied threat struck as cold as the glacial air, and Ross tried to meet it with an outward show of uncracked defenses. He decided to pick and choose from his information, feeding them scraps to stave off the inevitable. Hope dies very hard, and Ross having been pushed into corners long before his work at the project, had had considerable training in verbal fencing with hostile authority. He would volunteer nothing . . . Let it be pulled from him reluctant word by word! He would spin it out as long as he could and hope that time might fight for him.

"You are an agent . . ."

Ross accepted this statement as one he would neither affirm nor deny.

"You came to spy under the cover of a barbarian trader," smoothly, without pause, the man changed language in mid-sentence, slipping from the Beaker speech into English.

But long experience in meeting the dangerous with an expression of complete lack of comprehension was Ross's weapon now. He stared somewhat stupidly at his interrogator with that bewildered, boyish look he had so long cultivated to bemuse enemies in his past.

Whether he could have held out long against the other's skill—for Ross possessed no illusions concerning the type of examiner he now faced—he was never to know. Perhaps the drastic interruption that occurred the next moment saved for Ross a measure of self-esteem.

There was a distant boom, hollow and thunderous. Underneath and around them the floor, walls, and ceiling of the room moved as if they had been pried from their setting of ice and were being rolled about by the exploring thumb and forefinger of some impatient giant.

13

ROSS SWAYED against a guard, was fended off, and
bounced against the wall as the man shouted words
Ross could not understand. A determined roar from
the leader brought a semblance of order, but it was
plain that they had not been expecting this. Ross was
hustled out of the room back to his cell. His guards
were opening the cell door when a second shock was
felt and he was thrust into safekeeping with no ceremony.

He half crouched against the questionable security
of the wall, waiting through two more twisting earth
waves, both of which were accompanied or preceded
by dull sounds. Bombing! That last wrench was really
bad. Ross found himself lying on the floor, feeling
tremors rippling along the earth. His stomach
knotted convulsively with a fear unlike any he had
known before. It was as if the very security of the
world had been jerked from under him.

But that last explosion—if it was an explosion—
appeared to be the end. Ross sat up gingerly after sev-

eral long moments during which no more shocks moved the floor and walls. A line of light marked the door, showing cracks where none had previously existed. Ross, not yet ready to try standing erect, was heading toward it on his hands and knees, when a sharp noise behind him brought him to a stop.

There was no light to see by, but he was certain that the scrape of metal against metal sounded from the far side of the wall. He crawled back and put his ear to the surface. Now he heard not only that scraping, but an undercurrent of clicks, chippings . . .

Under his exploring hands the surface remained as smooth as ever, however. Then suddenly, perhaps a foot from his head, there sounded a rip of metal. The wall was being holed from the other side! Ross caught a flicker of very weak light, and moving in it was the point of a tool pulling at the smooth surface of the wall. It broke away with a brittle sound, and a hand holding a light reached through the aperture.

Ross wondered if he should catch that wrist, but the hope that the digger might just possibly be an ally kept him motionless. After the hand with the light whipped back beyond the wall, a wide section gave away and a hunched figure crawled through, followed by a second. In the limited glow he saw the first tunneler clearly enough.

"Assha!"

Ross was unprepared for what followed his cry. The lean brown man moved with a panther's striking speed, and Ross was forced back. A hand like a steel ring on his throat shut the breath away from his bursting lungs; the other's muscular body held him flat in spite of his struggles. The light of the small flash glowed inches beyond his eyes as he fought to fill his lungs. Then the hand on his throat was gone and he gasped, a little dizzy.

"Murdock! What are you doing—?" Ashe's clipped voice was muffled by another sudden explosion. This time the earth tremors not only hurled them from their feet, but seemed to run along the walls and across the ceiling. Ross, burying his face in the crook of his arm, could not rid himself of the fear that the building was being slowly twisted into scrap. When the shock was over he raised his head.

"What's going on?" He heard McNeil ask.

"Attack." That was Ashe. "But why, and by whom —don't ask me! You are a prisoner, I suppose, Murdock?"

"Yes, sir." Ross was glad that his voice sounded normal enough.

He heard someone sigh and guessed it was McNeil. "Another digging party." There was tired disgust in that.

"I don't understand," Ross appealed to that section of the dark where Ashe had been. "Have you been here all the time? Are you trying to dig your way out? I don't see how you can cut out of this glacier that we're parked under—"

"Glacier!" Ashe's exclamation was as explosive as the tremors. "So we're inside a glacier! That explains it. Yes, we've been here—"

"On ice!" McNeil commented and then laughed. "Glacier—ice—that's right, isn't it?"

"We're collaborating," Ashe continued. "Supplying our dear friends with a lot of information they already have and some flights of fancy they never dreamed about. However, they didn't know we had a few surprise packets of our own strewn about. It's amazing what the boys back at the project can pack away in a belt, or between layers of hide in a boot. So we've been engaged in some research of our own—"

"But I didn't have any escape gadgets." Ross was struck by the unfairness of that.

"No," Ashe agreed, his voice even and cold, "they are not entrusted to first-run men. You might slip up and use them at the wrong moment. However, you appear to have done fairly well . . ."

The heat of Ross's rising anger was chilled by the noise which cracked over their heads, ground to them through the walls, flattened and threatened them. He had thought those first shocks the end of this ice burrow and the world; he *knew* that this one was.

And the silence that followed was as threatening in its way as the clamor had been. Then there was a shout, a shriek. The space of light near the cell door was widening as that barrier, broken from its lock, swung open slowly. The fear of being trapped sent the men in that direction.

"Out!"

Ross was ready enough to respond to that order, but they were stopped by a crackle of sound that could be only one thing—rapid-fire guns. Somewhere in this warren a fight was in progress. Ross, remembering the arrogant face of the bald ship's officer, wondered if this was not an attack in force—the aliens against the looting Reds. If so, would the ship people distinguish between those found here. He feared not.

The room outside was clear, but not for long. As they lay watching, two men backed in, then whirled to stare at each other. A voice roared from beyond as if ordering them back to some post. One of them took a step forward in reluctant obedience, but the other grabbed his arm and pulled him away. They turned to run, and an automatic cracked.

The man nearest Ross gave a queer little cough and folded forward to his knees, sprawling on his face. His companion stared at him wildly for an instant, and then skidded into the passage beyond, escaping by inches a shot which clipped the door as he lunged through it.

No one followed, for outside there was a crescendo of noise—shouting, cries of pain, an unidentifiable hissing. Ashe darted into the room, taking cover by the body. Then he came back, the fellow's gun in his hand, and with a jerk of his head summoned the other two. He motioned them on in a direction away from the sounds of battle.

"I don't get all this," McNeil commented as they reached the next passage. "What's going on? Mutiny? Or have our boys gotten through?"

"It must be the ship people," Ross answered.

"What ship?" Ashe caught him up swiftly.

"The big one the Reds have been looting—"

"Ship?" echoed McNeil. "And *where* did you get that rig?" In the bright light it was easy to see Ross's alien dress. McNeil fingered the elastic material wonderingly.

"From the ship," Ross returned impatiently. "But if the ship people are attacking, I don't think they will notice any difference between us and the Reds . . ."

There was a burst of ear-splitting sound. For the third time Ross was thrown from his feet. This time the burrow lights flickered, dimmed, and went out.

"Oh, fine," commented McNeil bitterly out of the dark. "I never did care for blindman's buff."

"The transfer plate—" Ross clung to his own plan of escape—"if we can reach that—"

The light which had served Ashe and McNeil in their tunneling clicked on. Since the earth shocks appeared to be over for a while, they moved on, with Ashe in the lead and McNeil bringing up the rear. Ross hoped Ashe knew the way. The sound of fighting had died out, so one side or the other must have gained the victory. They might have only a few moments left to pass undetected.

Ross's sense of direction was fairly acute, but he could not have gone so unerringly to what he sought as Ashe did. Only he did not lead them to the room with the glowing plate, and Ross stifled a protest as they came instead to a small record room.

On a table were three spools of tape which Ashe caught up avidly, thrusting two in the front of his baggy tunic, passing the third to McNeil. Then he sped about trying the cupboards on the walls, but all were locked. His hand falling from the last latch, Ashe came back to the door where Ross waited.

"To the plate!" Ross urged.

Ashe surveyed the cupboards once more regretfully. "If we could have just ten minutes here—"

McNeil snorted. "Listen, you may yearn to be the filling in an ice sandwich, but I don't! Another shock and we'll be buried so deep even a drill couldn't find us. Let's get out now. The kid is right about that—if we still can."

Once more Ashe took the lead and they wove through ghostly rooms to what must have been the heart of the post—the transfer point. To Ross's unvoiced relief the plate was glowing. He had been nagged by the fear that when the lights blew out the transfer plate might also have been affected. He jumped for the plate.

Neither Ashe nor McNeil wasted time in joining him there. As they clung together there was a cry from behind them, underlined by a shot. Ross, feeling

Ashe sag against him, caught him in his arms. By the reflected glow of the plate he saw the Red leader of the post and behind him, his hairless face hanging oddly bodiless in the gloom, was the alien. Were those two now allies? Before Ross could be sure that he had really seen them, the wracking of space time caught him and the rest of the room faded away.

". . . free. Get a move on!"

Ross glanced across Ashe's bowed shoulders to McNeil's excited face. The other was pulling at Ashe, who was only half-conscious. A stream of blood from a hole in his bare shoulder soaked the upper edge of his Beaker tunic, but as they steadied him between them, he gained some measure of awareness and moved his feet as they pulled him off the plate.

Well, they were free if only for a few seconds, and there was no reception committee waiting for them. Ross gave thanks silently for those two small favors. But if they were now returned to the Bronze Age village, they were still in enemy territory. With Ashe wounded, the odds against them were so high it was almost hopeless.

Working hurriedly with strips torn from McNeil's kilt, they managed to stop the flow of blood from Ashe's wound. Although he was still groggy, he was fighting, driven by the fear which whipped them all— time was one of their foremost enemies. Ross, Ashe's gun in hand, kept watch on the transfer plate, ready to shoot at anything appearing there.

"That will have to do!" Ashe pulled free from McNeil. "We must move." He hesitated, and then pulling the spools of tape from his bloodstained tunic, passed them to McNeil. "You'd better carry these."

"All right," the other answered almost absently.

"Move!" The force of that order from Ashe sent

them into the corridor beyond. "The plate . . ." But the plate remained clear. And Ross noted that they must have returned to the proper time, for the walls about them were the logs and stone of the village he remembered.

"Someone coming through?"

"Should be—soon."

They fled, the hide boots of the other two making only the faintest whisper of sound, Ross's foam-soled feet none at all. He could not have found the door to the outer world, but again Ashe guided them, and only once did they have to seek cover. At last they faced a barred door. Ashe leaned against the wall, McNeil supporting him, as Ross pulled free the locking beam. They let themselves out into the night.

"Which way?" McNeil asked.

To Ross's surprise Ashe did not turn to the gate in the outer stockade. Instead he gestured at the mountain wall in the opposite direction. "They'll expect us to try for the valley pass. So we had better go up the slope there."

"That has the look of a tough climb," ventured McNeil.

Ashe stirred. "When it becomes too tough for me" —his voice was dry—"I shall say so, never fear."

He started out with some of his old ease of movement, but his companions closed in on either side, ready to offer aid. Ross often wondered later if they could have won free of the village on their own efforts that night. He was sure their resolution would have been equal to the attempt, but their escape would have depended upon a fabulous run of luck such as men seldom encounter.

As it was, they had just reached a pool of shadow beside a small hut some two buildings away from the one they had fled, when the fireworks began. As if on signal the three fugitives threw themselves flat. From the roof of the building at the center of the village a pencil of brilliant-green light pointed straight up into the sky, and around that spear of radiance the roof sprouted tongues of more natural red-and-yellow flames. Figures shot from doors as the fire lapped down the peak of the roof.

"Now!" In spite of the rising clamor, Ashe's voice carried to his two companions.

The three sprinted for the palisade, mingling with bewildered men who ran out of the other cabins. The waves of fire washed on, providing light, too much light. Ashe and McNeil could pass as part of the crowd, but Ross's unusual clothing might be easily marked.

Others were running for the wall. Ross and McNeil boosted Ashe to the top, saw him over in safety. McNeil followed. Ross was just reaching to draw himself up when he was enveloped in a beam of light.

A high, screeching call, unlike any shout he had heard, split the clamor. Frantically Ross tried for a hold, knowing that he was presenting a perfect target for those behind. He gained the top of the stockade, looked down into a black block of shadow, not knowing whether Ashe and McNeil were waiting for him or had gone ahead. Hearing that strange cry again, Ross leaped blindly out into the darkness.

He landed badly, hitting hard enough to bruise, but thanks to the skill he had learned for parachuting, he broke no bones. He got to his feet and blundered on in the general direction of the mountain Ashe had picked as their goal. There were others coming over the wall of the village and moving through the shadows, so he dared not call out for fear of alerting the enemy.

The village had been set in the widest part of the

valley. Behind its stockade the open ground narrowed swiftly, like the point of a funnel, and all fugitives from the settlement had to pass through that channel to escape. Ross's worst fear was that he had lost contact with Ashe and McNeil, and that he would never be able to pick up their trail in the wilderness ahead.

Thankful for the dark suit he wore which was protective covering in the night, he twice ducked into the brush to allow parties of refugees to pass him. Hearing them speak the guttural clicking speech he had learned from Ulffa's people, Ross deduced that they were innocent of the village's real purpose. These people were convinced they had been attacked by night demons. Perhaps there had only been a handful of Reds in that hidden retreat.

Ross pulled himself up a hard climb, and pausing to catch his breath, looked back. He was not overly surprised to see figures moving leisurely about the village examining the cabins, perhaps in search of the inhabitants. Each of those searchers was clad in a form-fitting suit that matched his own, and their bulbous hairless heads gleamed white in the firelight. Ross was astonished to see that they passed straight through the walls of flame, apparently unconcerned and unsinged by the heat.

The human beings trapped in the town wailed and ran, or lay and beat their heads and hands on the ground, supine before the invaders. Each captive was dragged back to a knot of aliens near the main building. Some were hurled out again into the dark, unharmed; a few others were retained. A sorting of prisoners was plainly in progress. There was no question that the ship people had followed through into this time, and that they had their own arrangements for the Reds.

Ross had no desire to learn the particulars. He started climbing again, finding the pass at last. Beyond, the ground fell away again, and Ross went forward into the full darkness of the night with a vast surge of thankfulness.

Finally, he stopped simply because he was too weary, too hungry, to keep on his feet without stumbling, and a fall in the dark on these heights could be costly. Ross discovered a small hollow behind a stunted tree and crept into it as best he could, his heart laboring against his ribs, a hot stab of pain cutting into his side with every breath he drew.

He awoke all at once with the snap of a fighting man who is alert to ever present danger. A hand lay warm and hard over his mouth, and above it his eyes met McNeil's. When he saw that Ross was awake McNeil withdrew his hand. The morning sunlight was warm about them. Moving clumsily because of his stiff, bruised body, Ross crawled out of the hollow. He looked around, but McNeil stood there alone. "Ashe?" Ross questioned him.

McNeil, showing a haggard face covered with several days' growth of rusty-brown beard, nodded his head toward the slope. Fumbling inside his kilt, he brought out something clenched in his fist and offered it to Ross. The latter held out his palm and McNeil covered it with a handful of coarse-ground grain. Just to look at the stuff made Ross long for a drink, but he mouthed it and chewed, getting up to follow McNeil down into the tree-grown lower slopes.

"It's not good." McNeil spoke jerkily, using Beaker speech. "Ashe is out of his head some of the time. That hole in his shoulder is worse than we thought it was, and there's always the threat of infection. This whole wood is full of people flushed out of that blasted village! Most of them—all I've seen—are natives. But they have it firmly planted in their minds now that there are devils after them. If they see you wearing that suit—"

"I know, and I'd strip if I could," Ross agreed. "But I'll have to get other clothing first; I can't run bare in this cold."

"That might be safer," McNeil growled. "I don't know just what happened back there, but it certainly must have been plenty!"

Ross swallowed a very dry mouthful of grain and then stopped to scoop up some leftover snow in the shadow of a tree root. It was not as refreshing as a real drink, but it helped. "You said Ashe is out of his head. What do we do for him, and what are your plans?"

"We have to reach the river, somehow. It drains to the sea, and at its mouth we are supposed to make contact with the sub."

The proposal sounded impossible to Ross, but so many impossible things had happened lately he was willing to go along with the idea—as long as he could. Gathering up more snow, he stuffed it into his mouth before he followed the already disappearing McNeil.

14

". . . THAT'S MY HALF of it. The rest of it you know."
Ross held his hands close to the small fire sheltered in
the pit he had helped dig and flexed his cold-numbed
fingers in the warmth.

From across the handful of flames Ashe's eyes, too
bright in a fever-flushed face, watched him demand-
ingly. The fugitives had taken cover in an angle where
the massed remains of an old avalanche provided a
cave-pocket. McNeil was off scouting in the gray
drizzle of the day, and their escape from the village
was now some forty-eight hours behind them.

"So the crackpots were right, after all. They only
had their times mixed." Ashe shifted on the bed of
brush and leaves they had raked together for his comfort.

"I don't understand—"

"Flying saucers," Ashe returned with an odd little
laugh. "It was a wild possibility, but it was on the
books from the start. This certainly will make Kelgarries turn red—"

"Flying saucers?"

Ashe must be out of his head from the fever, Ross

161

supposed. He wondered what he should do if Ashe tried to get up and walk away. He could not tackle a man with a bad hole in his shoulder, nor was he certain he could wrestle Ashe down in a real fight.

"That globe-ship was never built on this world. Use your head, Murdock. Think about your furry-faced friend and the baldy with him. Did either look like normal Terrans to you?"

"But—a spaceship!" It was something that had so long been laughed to scorn. When men had failed to break into space after the initial excitement of the satellite launchings, space flight had become a matter for jeers. On the other hand, there was the evidence collected by his own eyes and ears, his own experience. The services of the lifeboat had been techniques outside of his experience.

"This was insinuated once"—Ashe was lying flat now, gazing speculatively up at the projection of logs and earth which made them a partial roof—"along with a lot of other bright ideas, by a gentleman named Charles Fort, who took a lot of pleasure in pricking what he considered to be vastly over-inflated scientific pomposity. He gathered together four book loads of reported incidents of unexplainable happenings which he dared the scientists of his day to explain. And one of his bright suggestions was that such phenomena as the vast artificial earthworks found in Ohio and Indiana were originally thrown up by space castaways to serve as SOS signals. An intriguing idea, and now perhaps we may prove it true."

"But if such spaceships were wrecked on this world, I still don't see why we didn't find traces of them in our own time."

"Because that wreck you explored was bedded in a glacial era. Do you have any idea how long ago that was, counting from our own time? There were at least three glacial periods—and we don't know in which one the Reds went visiting. That age began about a million years before we were born, and the last of the ice ebbed out of New York State some thirty-eight thousand years ago, boy. That was the early Stone Age, reckoning it by the scale of human development, with an extremely thin population of the first real types of man clinging to a few warmer fringes of wilderness.

"Climatic changes, geographical changes, all altered the face of our continents. There was a sea in Kansas; England was part of Europe. So, even though as many as fifty such ships were lost here, they could all have been ground to bits by the ice flow, buried miles deep in quakes, or rusted away generations before the first really intelligent man arrived to wonder at them. Certainly there couldn't be too many such wrecks to be found. What do you think this planet was, a flypaper to attract them?"

"But if ships crashed here once, why didn't they later when men were better able to understand them?" Ross countered.

"For several reasons—all of them possible and able to be fitted into the fabric of history as we know it on this world. Civilizations rise, exist, and fall, each taking with it into the limbo of forgotten things some of the discoveries which made it great. How did the Indian civilizations of the New World learn to harden gold into a usable point for a cutting weapon? What was the secret of building possessed by the ancient Egyptians? Today you will find plenty of men to argue these problems and half a hundred others.

"The Egyptians once had a well-traveled trade route to India. Bronze Age traders opened up roads down into Africa. The Romans knew China. Then came an end to each of these empires, and those trade routes were forgotten. To our European ancestors of the Middle Ages, China was almost a legend, and the fact that the Egyptians had successfully sailed around the Cape of Good Hope was unknown. Suppose our space voyagers represented some star-born confederacy or empire which lived, rose to its highest point, and fell again into planet-bound barbarism all before the first of our species painted pictures on a cave wall?

"Or take it that this world was an unlucky reef on which too many ships and cargoes were lost, so that our whole solar system was posted, and skippers of star ships thereafter avoided it? Or they might even have had some rule that when a planet developed a primitive race of its own, it was to be left strictly alone until it discovered space flight for itself."

"Yes." Every one of Ashe's suppositions made good sense, and Ross was able to believe them. It was easier to think that both Furry-face and Baldy were inhabitants of another world than to think their kind existed on this planet before his own species was born. "But how did the Reds locate that ship?"

"Unless the information is on the tapes we were able to bring along, we shall probably never know," Ashe said drowsily. "I might make one guess—the Reds have been making an all-out effort for the past hundred years to open up Siberia. In some sections of that huge country there have been great climatic changes almost overnight in the far past. Mammoths have been discovered frozen in the ice with half-digested tropical plants in their stomach. It's as if the beasts were given some deep-freeze treatment instantaneously. If in their excavations the Reds came across the remains of a spaceship, remains well enough preserved for them to realize what they had discovered, they might start questing back in time to find a better one intact at an earlier date. That theory fits everything we know now."

"But why would the aliens attack the Reds now?"

"No ship's officers ever thought gently of pirates." Ashe's eyes closed.

There were questions, a flood of them, that Ross wanted to ask. He smoothed the fabric on his arm, that stuff which clung so tightly to his skin yet kept him warm without any need for more covering. If Ashe were right, on what world, what kind of world, had that material been woven, and how far had it been brought that he could wear it now?

Suddenly McNeil slid into their shelter and dropped two hares at the edge of the fire.

"How goes it?" he said, as Ross began to clean them.

"Reasonably well," Ashe, his eyes still closed, replied to that before Ross could. "How far are we from the river? And do we have company?"

"About five miles—if we had wings." McNeil answered in a dry tone. "And we have company all right, lots of it!"

That brought Ashe up, leaning forward on his good elbow. "What kind?"

"Not from the village." McNeil frowned at the fire which he fed with economic handfuls of sticks. "Something's happening on the side of the mountains. It looks as if there's a mass migration in progress. I counted five family clans on their way west —all in just this one morning."

"The village refugees' stories about devils might send them packing," Ashe mused.

"Maybe." But McNeil did not sound convinced. "The sooner we head downstream, the better. And I hope the boys will have that sub waiting where they promised. We do possess one thing in our favor—the spring floods are subsiding."

"And the high water should have plenty of raft material." Ashe lay back again. "We'll make those five miles tomorrow."

McNeil stirred uneasily and Ross, having cleaned and spitted the hares, swung them over the flames to broil. "Five miles in this country," the younger man observed, "is a pretty good day's march"—he did not add as he wanted to—"for a well man."

"I will make it," Ashe promised, and both listeners knew that as long as his body would obey him he meant to keep that promise. They also knew the futility of argument.

Ashe proved to be a prophet to be honored on two counts. They did make the trek to the river the next day, and there was a wealth of raft material marking the high-water level of the spring flood. The migrations McNeil had reported were still in progress, and the three men hid twice to watch the passing of small family clans. Once a respectably sized tribe, including wounded men, marched across their route, seeking a ford at the river.

"They've been badly mauled," McNeil whispered as they watched the people huddled along the water's edge while scouts cast upstream and down, searching for a ford. When they returned with the news that there was no ford to be found, the tribesmen then sullenly went to work with flint axes and knives to make rafts.

"Pressure—they are on the run." Ashe rested his chin on his good forearm and studied the busy scene. "These are not from the village. Notice the dress and the red paint on their faces. They're not like Ulffa's kin either. I wouldn't say they were local at all."

"Reminds me of something I saw once—animals running before a forest fire. They can't all be looking for new hunting territory," McNeil returned.

"Reds sweeping them out," Ross suggested. "or could the ship people—?"

Ashe started to shake his head and then winced. "I wonder . . ." The crease between his level brows deepened. "The ax people!" His voice was still a whisper, but it carried a note of triumph as if he had fitted some stubborn jigsaw piece into its proper place.

"Ax people?"

"Invasion of another people from the east. They turned up in prehistory about this period. Remember, Webb spoke of them. They used axes for weapons and tamed horses."

"Tartars"—McNeil was puzzled—"This far west?"

"Not Tartars, no. You needn't expect those to come boiling out of middle Asia for some thousands of years yet. We don't know too much about the ax people, save that they moved west from the interior plains. Eventually they crossed to Britain; perhaps they were the ancestors of the Celts who loved horses too. But in their time they were a tidal wave."

"The sooner we head downstream, the better." McNeil stirred restlessly, but they knew that they must keep to cover until the tribesmen below were gone. So they lay in hiding another night, witnessing on the next morning the arrival of a smaller party of the red-painted men, again with wounded among them. At the coming of this rear guard the activity on the river bank rose close to frenzy.

The three men out of time were doubly uneasy. It was not for them to merely cross the river. They had to build a raft which would be water-worthy enough to take them downstream—to the sea if they were lucky. And to build such a sturdy raft would take time, time they did not have now.

In fact, McNeil waited only until the last tribal raft was out of bow shot before he plunged down to the shore, Ross at his heels. Since they lacked even the stone tools of the tribesmen, they were at a disadvantage, and Ross found he was hands and feet for Ashe, working under the other's close direction. Before night closed in they had a good beginning and two sets of blistered hands, as well as aching backs.

When it was too dark to work any longer, Ashe pointed back over the track they had followed. Marking the mountain pass was a light. It looked like fire, and if it was, it must be a big one for them to be able to sight it across this distance.

"Camp?" McNeil wondered.

"Must be," Ashe agreed. "Those who built that blaze are in such numbers that they don't have to take precautions."

"Will they be here by tomorrow?"

"Their scouts might, but this is early spring, and forage can't have been too good on the march. If I were the chief of that tribe, I'd turn aside into the meadow land we skirted yesterday and let the herds graze for a day, maybe more. On the other hand, if they need water—"

"They will come straight ahead!" McNeil finished grimly. "And we can't be here when they arrive."

Ross stretched, grimacing at the twinge of pain in his shoulders. His hands smarted and throbbed, and this was just the beginning of their task. If Ashe had been fit, they might have trusted to logs for support and swum downstream to hunt a safer place for their shipbuilding project. But he knew that Ashe could not stand such an effort.

Ross slept that night mainly because his body was too exhausted to let him lie awake and worry. Roused in the earliest dawn by McNeil, they both crawled down to the water's edge and struggled to bind stubbornly resisting saplings together with cords twisted from bark. They reinforced them at crucial points with some strings torn from their kilts, and strips of rabbit hide saved from their kills of the past few days. They worked with hunger gnawing at them, having no time now to hunt. When the sun was well westward they had a clumsy craft which floated sluggishly. Whether it would answer to either pole or improvised paddle, they could not know until they tried it.

Ashe, his face flushed and his skin hot to the touch, crawled on board and lay in the middle, on the thin heap of bedding they had put there for him. He eagerly drank the water they carried to him in cupped hands and gave a little sigh of relief as Ross wiped his face with wet grass, muttering something about Kelgarries which neither of his companions understood.

McNeil shoved off and the bobbing craft spun around dizzily as the current pulled it free from the shore. They made a brave start, but luck deserted them before they had gotten out of sight of the spot where they embarked.

Striving to keep them in mid-current, McNeil poled furiously, but there were too many rocks and snagged trees with them, and coming up fast, was a full-sized tree. Twice its mat of branches caught on some snag, holding it back, and Ross breathed a little more freely, but it soon tore free again and rolled on, as menacing as a battering ram.

"Get closer to shore!" Ross shouted the warning. Those great, twisted roots seemed aimed straight at the raft, and he was sure if that mass struck them fairly, they would not have a chance. He dug in with his own pole, but his hasty push did not meet bottom; the stake in his hands plunged into some pothole in the hidden river bed. He heard McNeil cry out as he toppled into the water, gasping as the murky liquid flooded his mouth, choking him.

Half dazed by the shock, Ross struck out instinctively. The training at the base had included swimming, but to fight water in a pool under controlled conditions was far different from fighting death in a river of icy water when one had already swallowed a sizable quantity of that flood.

Ross had a half glimpse of a dark shadow. Was it the edge of the raft? He caught at it desperately, skinning his hands on rough bark, dragged on by it. The tree! He blinked his eyes to clear them of water, to try to see. But he could not pull his exhausted body high enough out of the water to see past the screen of roots; he could only cling to the small safety he had won and hope that he could rejoin the raft somewhere downstream.

After what seemed like a very long time he wedged one arm between two water-washed roots, sure that the support would hold his head above the surface. The chill of the stream struck at his hands and head, but the protection of the alien clothing was still effective, and the rest of his body was not cold. He was simply too tired to wrest himself free and trust again to the haphazard chance of making shore through the gathering dusk.

Suddenly a shock jarred his body and strained the arm he had thrust among the roots, wringing a cry out of him. He swung around and brushed footing under the water; the tree had caught on a shore snag. Pulling loose from the roots, he floundered on his hands and knees, falling afoul of a mass of reeds whose roots were covered with stale-smelling mud.

Like a wounded animal he dragged himself through the ooze to higher land, coming out upon an open meadow flooded with moonlight.

For a while he lay there, his cold, sore hands under him, plastered with mud and too tired to move. The sound of a sharp barking aroused him—an imperative, summoning bark, neither belonging to a wolf nor a hunting fox. He listened to it dully and then, through the ground upon which he lay, Ross felt as well as heard the pounding of hoofs.

Hoofs—horses! Horses from over the mountains—horses which might mean danger. His mind seemed as dull and numb as his hands, and it took quite a long time for him to fully realize the menace horses might bring.

Getting up, Ross noticed a winged shape sweeping across the disk of the moon like a silent dart. There was a single despairing squeak out of the grass about a hundred feet away, and the winged shape arose again with its prey. Then the barking sound once more—eager, excited barking.

Ross crouched back on his heels and saw a smoky brand of light moving along the edge of the meadow where the band of trees began. Could it be a herd guard? Ross knew he had to head back toward the river, but he had to force himself on the path, for he did not know whether he dared enter the stream again. But what would happen if they hunted him with the dog? Confused memories of how water spoiled scent spurred him on.

Having reached the rising bank he had climbed so laboriously before, Ross miscalculated and tumbled back, rolling down into the mud of the reed bed. Mechanically he wiped the slime from his face. The tree was still anchored there; by some freak the current had rammed its rooted end up on a sand spit.

Above in the meadow the barking sounded very close and now it was answered by a second canine belling. Ross wormed his way back through the reeds to the patch of water between the tree and the bank. His few poor efforts at escape were almost half-consciously taken; he was too tired to really care now.

Soon he saw a four-footed shape running along the top of the bank, giving tongue. It was then joined by a larger and even more vocal companion. The dogs drew even with Ross, who wondered dully if the animals could sight him in the shadows below, or whether they only scented his presence. Had he been able, he would have climbed over the log and taken his chances in the open water, but now he could only lie where he was—the tangle of roots between him and the bank serving as a screen, which would be little enough protection when men came with torches.

Ross was mistaken, however, for his worm's progress across the reed bed had liberally besmeared his dark clothing and masked the skin of his face and hands, giving him better cover than any he could have wittingly devised. Though he felt naked and defenseless, the men who trailed the hounds to the river bank, thrusting out the torch over the edge to light the sand spit, saw nothing but the trunk of the tree wedged against a mound of mud.

Ross heard a confused murmur of voices broken by the clamor of the dogs. Then the torch was raised out of line of his dazzled eyes. He saw one of the indistinct figures above cuff away a dog and move off, calling the hounds after it. Reluctantly, still barking, the animals went. Ross, with a little sob, subsided limply in the uncomfortable net of roots, still undiscovered.

15

IT WAS such a small thing, a tag of ragged stuff looped about a length of splintered sapling. Ross climbed stiffly over the welter of drift caught on the sand spit and pulled it loose, recognizing the string even before he touched it. That square knot was of McNeil's tying, and as Murdock sat down weakly in the sand and mud, nervously fingering the twisted cord, staring vacantly at the river, his last small hope died. The raft must have broken up, and neither Ashe nor McNeil could have survived the ultimate disaster.

Ross Murdock was alone, marooned in a time which was not his own, with little promise of escape. That one thought blanked out his mind with its own darkness. What was the use of getting up again, of trying to find food for his empty stomach, or warmth and shelter?

He had always prided himself on being able to go it alone, had thought himself secure in that calculated loneliness. Now that belief had been washed away in the river along with most of the will power which had kept him going these past days. Before, there had always been some goal, no matter how remote. Now, he had nothing. Even if he managed to reach the mouth of the river, he had no idea of where or how to summon the sub from the overseas post. All three of the time travelers might already have been written off the rolls, since they had not reported in.

Ross pulled the rag free from the sapling and wreathed it in a tight bracelet about his grimed wrist for some unexplainable reason. Worn and tired, he tried to think ahead. There was no chance of again contacting Ulffa's tribe. Alone with all the other woodland hunters they must have fled before the advance of the horsemen. No, there was no reason to go back, and why make the effort to advance?

The sun was hot. This was one of those spring days which foretell the ripeness of summer. Insects buzzed in the reed banks where a green sheen showed. Birds wheeled and circled in the sky, some flock disturbed, their cries reaching Ross in hoarse calls of warning.

He was still plastered with patches of dried mud and slime, the reek of it thick in his nostrils. Now Ross brushed at a splotch on his knee, picking loose flakes to expose the alien cloth of his suit underneath, seemingly unbefouled. All at once it became necessary to be clean again at least.

Ross waded into the stream, stooping to splash the brown water over his body and then rubbing away the resulting mud. In the sunlight the fabric had a brilliant glow, as if it not only drew the light but reflected it. Wading farther out into the water, he began to swim, not with any goal in view, but because it was easier than crawling back to land once more.

Using the downstream current to supplement his skill, he watched both banks. He could not really hope to see either the raft or indications that its passengers had won to shore, but somewhere deep inside him he had not yet accepted the probable.

The effort of swimming broke through that fog of inertia which had held him since he had awakened that morning. It was with a somewhat healthier interest in life that Ross came ashore again on an arm of what was a bay or inlet angling back into the land. Here the banks of the river were well above his head, and believing that he was well sheltered, he stripped, hanging his suit in the sunlight and letting the unusual heat of the day soothe his body.

A raw fish, cornered in the shallows and scooped out, furnished one of the best meals he had ever tasted. He had reached for the suit draped over a willow limb when the first and only warning that his fortunes had once again changed came, swiftly, silently, and with deadly promise.

One moment the willows had moved gently in the breeze, and then a spear suddenly set them all quivering. Ross clutching the suit to him with a frantic grab, skated about in the sand, going to one knee in his haste.

He found himself completely at the mercy of the two men standing on the bank well above him. Unlike Ulffa's people or the Beaker traders, they were very tall, with heavy braids of light or sun-bleached hair swinging forward on their wide chests. Their leather tunics hung to mid-thigh above leggings which were bound to their limbs with painted straps. Cuff bracelets of copper ringed their forearms, and necklaces of animal teeth and beads displayed their personal wealth. Ross could not remember having seen their like on any of the briefing tapes at the base.

One spear had been a warning, but a second was

held ready, so Ross made the age-old signal of surrender, reluctantly dropping his suit and raising his hands palm out and shoulder high.

"Friend?" Ross asked in the Beaker tongue. The traders ranged far, and perhaps there was a chance they had had contact with this tribe.

The spear twirled, and the younger stranger effortlessly leaped down the bank, paddling over to Ross to pick up the suit he had dropped, holding it up while he made some comment to his companion. He seemed fascinated by the fabric, pulling and smoothing it between his hands, and Ross wondered if there was a chance of trading it for his own freedom.

Both men were armed, not only with the long-bladed daggers favored by the Beaker folk, but also with axes. When Ross made a slight effort to lower his hands the man before him reached to his belt ax, growling what was plainly a warning. Ross blinked, realizing that they might well knock him out and leave him behind, taking the suit with them.

Finally, they decided in favor of including him in their loot. Throwing the suit over one arm, the stranger caught Ross by the shoulder and pushed him forward roughly. The pebbled beach was painful to Ross's feet, and the breeze which whipped about him as he reached the top of the bank reminded him only too forcibly of his ordeal in the glacial world.

Murdock was tempted to make a sudden dash out on the point of the bank and dive into the river, but it was already too late. The man who was holding the spear had moved behind him, and Ross's wrist, held in a vise grip at the small of his back, kept him prisoner as he was pushed on into the meadow. There three shaggy horses grazed, their nose ropes gathered into the hands of a third man.

A sharp stone half buried in the ground changed the pattern of the day. Ross's heel scraped against it, and the resulting pain triggered his rebellion into explosion. He threw himself backward, his bruised heel sliding between the feet of his captor, bringing them both to the ground with himself on top. The other expelled air from his lungs in a grunt of surprise, and Ross whipped over, one hand grasping the hilt of the tribesman's dagger while the other, free of that prisoning wristlock, chopped at the fellow's throat.

Dagger out and ready, Ross faced the men in a half crouch as he had been drilled. They stared at him in open-mouthed amazement, then too late the spears went up. Ross placed the point of his looted weapon at the throat of the now quiet man by whom he knelt, and he spoke the language he had learned from Ulffa's people.

"You strike—this one dies."

They must have read the determined purpose in his eyes, for slowly, reluctantly, the spears went down. Having gained so much of a victory, Ross dared more. "Take—" he motioned to the waiting horses— "take and go!"

For a moment he thought that this time they would meet his challenge, but he continued to hold the dagger above the brown throat of the man who was now moaning faintly. His threat continued to register, for the other man shrugged the suit from his arm, left it lying on the ground, and retreated. Holding the nose rope of his horse, he mounted, waved the herder up also, and both of them rode slowly away.

The prisoner was slowly coming around, so Ross only had time to pull on the suit; he had not even fastened the breast studs before those blue eyes opened. A sunburned hand flashed to a belt, but the dagger and ax which had once hung there were now in Ross's possession. He watched the tribesman carefully as he finished dressing.

"What you do?" The words were in the speech of the forest people, distorted by a new accent.

"You go—" Ross pointed to the third horse the others had left behind—"I go—" he indicated the river—"I take these"—he patted the dagger and the ax. The other scowled.

"Not good . . ."

Ross laughed, a little hysterically. "Not good you," he agreed, "good—me!"

To his surprise the tribesman's stiff face relaxed, and the fellow gave a bark of laughter. He sat up, rubbing at his throat, a big grin pulling at the corners of his mouth.

"You hunter?" The man pointed northeast to the woodlands fringing the mountains.

Ross shook his head. "Trader, me."

"Trader," the other repeated. Then he tapped one of the wide metal cuffs at his wrist. "Trade—this?"

"That. More things."

"Where?"

Ross pointed downstream. "By bitter water—trade there."

The man appeared puzzled. "Why you here?"

"Ride river water, like you ride," he said, pointing to the horse. "Ride on trees—many trees tied together. Trees break apart—I come here."

The conception of a raft voyage apparently got across, for the tribesman was nodding. Getting to his feet, he walked across to take up the nose rope of the waiting horse. "You come camp—Foscar. Foscar chief. He like you show trick how you take Tulka, make him sleep—hold his ax, knife."

Ross hesitated. This Tulka seemed friendly now, but would that friendliness last? He shook his head. "I go to bitter water. My chief there."

Tulka was scowling again. "You speak crooked words—your chief there!" He pointed eastward with a dramatic stretch of the arm. "You chief speak Foscar. Say he give much these—" he touched his copper cuffs—"good knives, axes—get you back."

Ross stared at him without understanding. Ashe? Ashe in this Foscar's camp offering a reward for him? But how could that be?

"How you know my chief?"

Tulka laughed, this time derisively. "You wear shining skin—your chief wear shiny skin. He say find other shiny skin—give many good things to man who bring you back."

Shiny skin! The suit from the alien ship! Was it the ship people? Ross remembered the light on him as he climbed out of the Red village. He must have been sighted by one of the spacemen. But why were they searching for him, alerting the natives in an effort to scoop him up? What made Ross Murdock so important that they must have him? He only knew that he was not going to be taken if he could help it, that he had no desire to meet this "chief" who had offered treasure for his capture.

"You will come!" Tulka went into action, his mount flashing forward almost in a running leap at Ross, who stumbled back when horse and rider loomed over him. He swung up the ax, but it was a weapon with which he had no training, too heavy for him.

As his blow met only thin air the shoulder of the mount hit him, and Ross went down, avoiding by less than a finger's breadth the thud of an unshod hoof against his skull. Then the rider landed on him, crushing him flat. A fist connected with his jaw, and for Ross the sun went out.

He found himself hanging across a support which moved with a rocking gait, whose pounding hurt his head, keeping him half dazed. Ross tried to move, but he realized that his arms were behind his back, fastened wrist to wrist, and a warm weight centered in the small of his spine to hold him face down on a horse. He could do nothing except endure the discomfort as best he could and hope for a speedy end to the gallop.

Over his head passed the cackle of speech. He caught short glimpses of another horse matching pace to the one that carried him. Then they swept into a noisy place where the shouting of many men made a din. The horse stopped and Ross was pulled from its back and dropped to the trodden dust, to lie blinking up dizzily, trying to focus on the scene about him.

They had arrived at the camp of the horsemen, whose hide tents served as a backdrop for the fair long-haired giants and the tall women hovering about to view the captive. The circle about him then broke, and men stood aside for a newcomer. Ross had believed that his original captors were physically imposing, but this one was their master. Lying on the ground at the chieftain's feet, Ross felt like a small and helpless child.

Foscar, if Foscar this was, could not yet have entered middle age, and the muscles which moved along his arms and across his shoulders as he leaned over to study Tulka's prize made him bear-strong. Ross glared up at him, that same hot rage which had led to his attack on Tulka now urging him to the only defiance he had left—words.

"Look well, Foscar. Free me, and I would do more than *look* at you," he said in the speech of the woods hunters.

Foscar's blue eyes widened and he lowered a fist which could have swallowed in its grasp both of Ross's hands, linking those great fingers in the stuff of the suit and drawing the captive to his feet, with no sign that his act had required any effort. Even standing, Ross was a good eight inches shorter than the chieftain. Yet he put up his chin and eyed the other squarely, without giving ground.

"So—yet still my hands are tied." He put into that all the taunting inflection he could summon. His reception by Tulka had given him one faint clue to the character of these people; they might be brought to acknowledge the worth of one who stood up to them.

"Child—" The fist shifted from its grip on the fabric covering Ross's chest to his shoulder, and now under its compulsion Ross swayed back and forth.

"Child?" From somewhere Ross raised that short laugh. "Ask Tulka. I be no child, Foscar. Tulka's ax, Tulka's knife—they were in my hand. A horse Tulka had to use to bring me down."

Foscar regarded him intently and then grinned. "Sharp tongue," he commented. "Tulka lost knife—ax? So! Ennar," he called over his shoulder, and one of the men stepped out a pace beyond his fellows.

He was shorter and much younger than his chief, with a boy's rangy slimness and an open, good-looking face, his eyes bright on Foscar with a kind of eager excitement. Like the other tribesmen he was armed with belt dagger and ax, and since he wore two necklaces and both cuff bracelets and upper armlets as did Foscar, Ross thought he must be a relative of the older man.

"Child!" Foscar clapped his hand on Ross's shoulder and then withdrew the hold. "Child!" He indicated Ennar, who reddened. "You take from Ennar ax, knife," Foscar ordered, "as you took from Tulka." He made a sign, and someone cut the thongs about Ross's wrists.

Ross rubbed one numbed hand against the other, setting his jaw. Foscar had stung his young follower with that contemptuous "child," so the boy would be eager to match all his skill against the prisoner. This would not be as easy as his taking Tulka by surprise. But if he refused, Foscar might well order him killed out of hand. He had chosen to be defiant; he would have to do his best.

"Take—ax, knife—" Foscar stepped back, waving at his men to open out a ring encircling the two young men.

Ross felt a little sick as he watched Ennar's hand go to the haft of the ax. Nothing had been said about Ennar's not using his weapons in defense, but Ross discovered that there was some sense of sportsmanship in the tribesmen, after all. It was Tulka who pushed to the chief's side and said something which made Foscar roar bull-voiced at his youthful companion.

Ennar's hand came away from the ax hilt as if that polished wood were white-hot, and he transferred his discomforture to Ross as the other understood. Ennar had to win now for his own pride's sake, and Ross felt *he* had to win for his life. They circled warily, Ross watching his opponent's eyes rather than those half-closed hands held at waist level.

Back at the base he had been matched with Ashe, and before Ashe with the tough-bodied, skilled, and merciless trainers in unarmed combat. He had had beaten into his bruised flesh knowledge of holds and blows intended to save his skin in just such an encounter. But then he had been well-fed, alert, prepared. He had not been knocked silly and then transported for miles slung across a horse after days of exposure and hard usage. It remained to be learned—was Ross Murdock as tough as he always thought himself to be? Tough or not, he was in this until he won—or dropped.

Comments from the crowd aroused Ennar to the first definite action. He charged, stooping low in a wrestler's stance, but Ross squatted even lower. One hand flicked to the churned dust of the ground and snapped up again, sending a cloud of grit into the tribesman's face. Then their bodies met with a shock, and Ennar sailed over Ross's shoulder to skid along the earth.

Had Ross been fresh, the contest would have ended there and then in his favor. But when he tried to whirl and throw himself on his opponent he was too slow. Ennar was not waiting to be pinned flat, and it was Ross's turn to be caught at a disadvantage.

A hand shot out to catch his leg just above the ankle, and once again Ross obeyed his teaching, falling easily at that pull, to land across his opponent. Ennar, disconcerted by the too-quick success of his attack, was unprepared for this. Ross rolled, trying to escape steel-fingered hands, his own chopping out in edgewise blows, striving to serve Ennar as he had Tulka.

He had to take a lot of punishment, though he managed to elude the powerful bear's hug in which he knew the other was laboring to engulf him, a hold which would speedily crush him into submission. Clinging to the methods he had been taught, he fought on, only now he knew, with a growing panic, that his best was not good enough. He was too spent to make an end. Unless he had some piece of great good luck, he could only delay his own defeat.

Fingers clawed viciously at his eyes, and Ross did what he had never thought to do in any fight—he snapped wolfishly, his teeth closing on flesh as he brought up his knee and drove it home into the body wriggling on his. There was a gasp of hot breath in his face as Ross called upon the last few rags of his strength, tearing loose from the other's slackened hold. He scrambled to one knee. Ennar was also on his knees, crouching like a four-legged beast ready to spring. Ross risked everything on a last gamble. Clasping his hands together, he raised them as high as he could and brought them down on the nape of the other's neck. Ennar sprawled forward facedown in the dust where seconds later Ross joined him.

16

MURDOCK LAY on his back, gazing up at the laced hides which stretched to make the tent roofing. Having been battered just enough to feel all one aching bruise, Ross had lost interest in the future. Only the present mattered, and it was a dark one. He might have fought Ennar to a standstill, but in the eyes of the horsemen he had also been beaten, and he had not impressed them as he had hoped. That he still lived was a minor wonder, but he deduced that he continued to breathe only because they wanted to exchange him for the reward offered by the aliens from out of time, an unpleasant prospect to contemplate.

His wrists were lashed over his head to a peg driven deeply into the ground; his ankles were bound to another. He could turn his head from side to side, but any further movement was impossible. He ate only bits of food dropped into his mouth by a dirty-fingered slave, a cowed hunter captured from a tribe overwhelmed in the migration of the horsemen.

"Ho—taker of axes!" A toe jarred into his ribs, and

Ross bit back the grunt of pain which answered that rude bid for his attention. He saw in the dim light Ennar's face and was savagely glad to note the discolorations about the right eye and along the jaw line, the signatures left by his own skinned knuckles.

"Ho—warrior!" Ross returned hoarsely, trying to lade that title with all the scorn he could summon.

Ennar's hand, holding a knife, swung into his limited range of vision. "To clip a sharp tongue is a good thing!" The young tribesman grinned as he knelt down beside the helpless prisoner.

Ross knew a thrill of fear worse than any pain. Ennar might be about to do just what he hinted! Instead, the knife swung up and Ross felt the sawing at the cords about his wrists, enduring the pain in the raw gouges they had cut in his flesh with gratitude that it was not mutilation which had brought Ennar to him. He knew that his arms were free, but to draw them down from over his head was almost more than he could do, and he lay quiet as Ennar loosed his feet.

"Up!"

Without Ennar's hands pulling at him, Ross could not have reached his feet. Nor did he stay erect once he had been raised, crashing forward on his face as the other let him go, hot anger eating at him because of his own helplessness.

In the end, Ennar summoned two slaves who dragged Ross into the open where a council assembled about a fire. A debate was in progress, sometimes so heated that the speakers fingered their knife or ax hilts when they shouted their arguments. Ross could not understand their language, but he was certain that he was the subject under discussion and that Foscar had the deciding vote and had not yet given the nod to either side.

Ross sat where the slaves had dumped him, rubbing his smarting wrists, so deathly weary in mind and beaten in body that he was not really interested in the fate they were planning for him. He was content merely to be free of his bonds, a small favor, but one he savored dully.

He did not know how long the debate lasted, but at length Ennar came to stand over him with a message. "Your chief—he give many good things for you. Foscar take you to him."

"My chief is not here," Ross repeated wearily, making a protest he knew they would not heed. "My chief sits by the bitter water and waits. He will be angry if I do not come. Let Foscar fear his anger—"

Ennar laughed. "You run from your chief. He will be happy with Foscar when you lie again under his hand. You will not like that—I think it so!"

"I think so, too," Ross agreed silently.

He spent the rest of that night lying between the watchful Ennar and another guard, though they had the humanity not to bind him again. In the morning he was allowed to feed himself, and he fished chunks of venison out of a stew with his unwashed fingers. But in spite of the messiness, it was the best food he had eaten in days.

The trip, however, was not to be a comfortable one. He was mounted on one of the shaggy horses, a rope run under the animal's belly to loop one foot to the other. Fortunately, his hands were bound so he was able to grasp the coarse, wiry mane and keep his seat after a fashion. The nose rope of his mount was passed to Tulka, and Ennar rode beside him with only half an eye for the path of his own horse and the balance of his attention for the prisoner.

They headed northeast, with the mountains as a

sharp green-and-white goal against the morning sky.
Though Ross's sense of direction was not too acute,
he was certain that they were making for the general
vicinity of the hidden village, which he believed the
ship people had destroyed. He tried to discover something of the nature of the contact which had been
made between the aliens and the horsemen.

"How find other chief?" he asked Ennar.

The young man tossed one of his braids back
across his shoulder and turned his head to face Ross
squarely. "Your chief come our camp. Talk with
Foscar—two—four sleeps ago."

"How talk with Foscar? With hunter talk?"

For the first time Ennar did not appear altogether
certain. He scowled and then snapped, "He talk—
Foscar, us. We hear right words—not woods creeper
talk. He speak to us good."

Ross was puzzled. How could the alien out of time
speak the proper language of a primitive tribe some
thousands of years removed from his own era? Were
the ship people also familiar with time travel? Did
they have their own stations of transfer? Yet their
fury with the Reds had been hot. This was a complete
mystery.

"This chief—he look like me?"

Again Ennar appeared at a loss. "He wear covering, like you."

"But was he like me?" persisted Ross. He didn't
know what he was trying to learn, only that it seemed
important at that moment to press home to at least
one of the tribesmen that he *was* different from the
man who had put a price on his head and to whom he
was to be sold.

"Not like!" Tulka spoke over his shoulder. "You
look like hunter people—hair, eyes—Strange chief no

hair on head, eyes not like—"

"You saw him too?" Ross demanded eagerly.

"I saw. I ride to camp—they come so. Stand on rock, call to Foscar. Make magic with fire—it jump up!" He pointed his arm stiffly at a bush before them on the trail. "They point little, little spear—fire come out of the ground and burn. They say burn our camp if we do not give them man. We say—not have man. Then they say many good things for us if we find and bring man—"

"But they are not my people," Ross cut in. "You see, I have hair, I am not like them. They are bad—"

"You may be taken in war by them—chief's slave." Ennar had a reply to that which was logical according to the customs of his own tribe. "They want slave back—it is so."

"My people strong too, much magic," Ross pushed. "Take me to bitter water and they pay much —more than stranger chief!"

Both tribesmen were amused. "Where bitter water?" asked Tulka.

Ross jerked his head to the west. "Some sleeps away—"

"Some sleeps!" repeated Ennar jeeringly. "We ride some sleeps, maybe many sleeps where we know not the trails—maybe no people there, maybe no bitter water—all things you say with split tongue so that we not give you back to master. We go this way not even one sleep—find chief, get good things. Why we do hard thing when we can do easy?"

What argument could Ross offer in rebuttal to the simple logic of his captors? For a moment he raged inwardly at his own helplessness. But long ago he had learned that giving away to hot fury was no good unless one did it deliberately to impress, and then only when one had the upper hand. Now Ross had no hand at all.

For the most part they kept to the open, whereas Ross and the other two agents had skulked in wooded areas on their flight through this same territory. So they approached the mountains from a different angle, and though he tried, Ross could pick out no familiar landmarks. If by some miracle he was able to free himself from his captors, he could only head due west and hope to strike the river.

At midday their party made camp in a grove of trees by a spring. The weather was as unseasonably warm as it had been the day before, and flies, brought out of cold-weather hiding, attacked the stamping horses and crawled over Ross. He tried to keep them off with swings of his bound hands, for their bites drew blood.

Having been tumbled from his mount, he remained fastened to a tree with a noose about his neck while the horsemen built a fire and broiled strips of deer meat.

It would seem that Foscar was in no hurry to get on, since after they had eaten, the men continued to lounge at ease, some even dropping off to sleep. When Ross counted faces he learned that Tulka and another had both disappeared, possibly to contact and warn the aliens they were coming.

It was midafternoon before the scouts reappeared, as unobtrusively as they had gone. They went before Foscar with a report which brought the chief over to Ross. "We go. Your chief waits—"

Ross raised his swollen, bitten face and made his usual protest. "Not my chief!"

Foscar shrugged. "He say so. He give good things to get you back under his hand. So—he your chief!"

Once again Ross was boosted on his mount, and bound. But this time the party split into two groups as they rode off. He was with Ennar again, just behind Foscar, with two other guards bringing up the rear. The rest of the men, leading their mounts, melted into the trees. Ross watched that quiet withdrawal speculatively. It argued that Foscar did not trust those he was about to do business with, that he was taking certain precautions of his own. Only Ross could not see how that distrust, which might be only ordinary prudence on Foscar's part, could in any way be an advantage for him.

They rode at a pace hardly above a walk into a small open meadow narrowing at the east. Then for the first time Ross was able to place himself. They were at the entrance to the valley of the village, about a mile away from the narrow throat above which Ross had lain to spy and had been captured, for he had come from the north over the spurs of rising ridges.

Ross's horse was pulled up as Foscar drove his heel into the ribs of his own mount, sending it at a brisker pace toward the neck of the valley. There was a blot of blue there—more than one of the aliens were waiting. Ross caught his lip between his teeth and bit down on it hard. He had stood up to the Reds, to Foscar's tribesmen, but he shrank from meeting those strangers with an odd fear that the worst the men of his own species could do would be but a pale shadow to the treatment he might meet at their hands.

Foscar was now a toy man astride a toy horse. He halted his galloping mount to sit facing the handful of strangers. Ross counted four of them. They seemed to be talking, though there was still a good distance separating the mounted man and the blue suits.

Minutes passed before Foscar's arm raised in a wave to summon the party guarding Ross. Ennar kicked his horse to a trot, towing Ross's mount behind, the other two men thudding along more discreetly. Ross noted that they were both armed with spears which they carried to the fore as they rode.

They were perhaps three quarters of the way to join Foscar, and Ross could see plainly the bald heads of the aliens as their faces turned in his direction. Then the strangers struck. One of them raised a weapon shaped similarly to the automatic Ross knew, except that it was longer in the barrel.

Ross did not know why he cried out, except that Foscar had only an ax and dagger which were both still sheathed at his belt. The chief sat very still, and then his horse gave a swift sidewise swerve as if in fright. Foscar collapsed, limp, bonelessly, to the trodden turf, to lie unmoving face down.

Ennar whooped, a cry combining defiance and despair in one. He reined up with violence enough to set his horse rearing. Then, dropping his hold on the leading rope of Ross's mount, he whirled and set off in a wild dash for the trees to the left. A spear lanced across Ross's shoulder, ripping at the blue fabric, but his horse whirled to follow the other, taking him out of danger of a second thrust. Having lost his opportunity, the man who had wielded the spear dashed by at Ennar's back.

Ross clung to the mane with both hands. His greatest fear was that he might slip from the saddle pad and since he was tied by his feet, lie unprotected and helpless under those dashing hoofs. Somehow he managed to cling to the horse's neck, his face lashed by the rough mane while the animal pounded on. Had Ross been able to grasp the dangling rope, he might have had a faint chance of controlling that run, but as it was he could only hold fast and hope.

He had only broken glimpses of what lay ahead. Then a brilliant fire, as vivid as the flames which had eaten up the Red village, burst from the ground a few yards ahead, sending the horse wild. There was more fire and the horse changed course through the rising smoke. Ross realized that the aliens were trying to cut him off from the thin safety of the woodlands. Why they didn't just shoot him as they had Foscar he could not understand.

The smoke of the burning grass was thick, cutting between him and the woods. Might it also provide a curtain behind which he could hope to escape both parties? The fire was sending the horse back toward the waiting ship people. Ross could hear a confused shouting in the smoke. Then his mount made a miscalculation, and a tongue of red licked too close. The animal screamed, dashing on blindly straight between two of the blazes and away from the blue-clad men.

Ross coughed, almost choking, his eyes watering as the stench of singed hair thickened the smoke. But he had been carried out of the fire circle and was shooting back into the meadow-land. Mount and unwilling rider were well away from the upper end of that cleared space when another horse cut in from the left, matching speed to the uncontrolled animal to which Ross clung. It was one of the tribesmen riding easily.

The trick worked, for the wild race slowed to a gallop and the other rider, in a feat of horsemanship at which Ross marveled, leaned from his seat to catch the dangling nose rope, bringing the runaway against his own steady steed. Ross shaken, still coughing from the smoke and unable to sit upright, held to the mane. The gallop slowed to a rocking pace and finally

came to a halt, both horses blowing, white-foam
patches on their chests and their riders' legs.

Having made his capture, the tribesman seemed in-
different to Ross, looking back instead at the wide
curtain of grass smoke, frowning as he studied the
swift spread of the fire. Muttering to himself, he
pulled the lead rope and brought Ross's horse to follow in the direction from which Ennar had brought
the captive less than a half hour earlier.

Ross tried to think. The unexpected death of their
chief might well mean his own, should the tribe's desire for vengeance now be aroused. On the other
hand, there was a faint chance that he could now better impress them with the thought that he was indeed
of another clan and that to aid him would be to work
against a common enemy.

But it was hard to plan clearly, though wits alone
could save him now. The parley which had ended
with Foscar's murder had brought Ross a small measure of time. He was still a captive, even though of the
tribesmen and not the unearthly strangers. Perhaps to
the ship people these primitives were hardly higher in
scale than the forest animals.

Ross did not try to talk to his present guard, who
towed him into the western sun of late afternoon.
They halted at last in that same small grove where
they had rested at noon. The tribesman fastened the
mounts and then walked around to inspect the animal
Ross had ridden. With a grunt he loosened the prisoner and spilled him unceremoniously on the ground
while he examined the horse. Ross levered himself up
to sight the mark of the burn across that roan hide
where the fire had blistered the skin.

Thick handfuls of mud from the side of the spring
were brought and plastered over the seared strip.

Then, having rubbed down both animals with twists of grass, the man came over to Ross, pushed him back to the ground, and studied his left leg.

Ross understood. By rights, his thigh should also have been scorched where the flame had hit, yet he felt no pain. Now as the tribesman examined him for a burn, he could not see even the faintest discoloration of the strange fabric. He remembered how the aliens had strolled unconcerned through the burning village. As the suit had insulated him against the cold of the ice, so it would seem that it had also protected him against the fire, for which he was duly thankful. His escape from injury was a puzzle to the tribesman, who, failing to find any trace of burn on him, left Ross alone and went to sit well away from his prisoner as if he feared him.

They did not have long to wait. One by one, those who had ridden in Foscar's company gathered at the grove. The very last to come were Ennar and Tulka, carrying the body of their chief. The faces of both men were smeared with dust and when the others sighted the body they, too, rubbed dust into their cheeks, reciting a string of words and going one by one to touch the dead chieftain's right hand.

Ennar, resigning his burden to the others, slid from his tired horse and stood for a long moment, his head bowed. Then he gazed straight at Ross and came across the tiny clearing to stand over the man of a later time. The boyishness which had been a part of him when he had fought at Foscar's command was gone. His eyes were merciless as he leaned down to speak, shaping each word with slow care so that Ross could understand the promise—that frightful promise:

"Woods rat, Foscar goes to his burial fire. And he

shall take a slave with him to serve him beyond the sky—a slave to run at his voice, to shake when he thunders. Slave-dog, you shall run for Foscar beyond the sky, and he shall have you forever to walk upon as a man walks upon the earth. I, Ennar, swear that Foscar shall be sent to the chiefs in the sky in all honor. And that you, dog-one, shall lie at his feet in that going!"

He did not touch Ross, but there was no doubt in Ross's mind that he meant every word he spoke.

17

THE PREPARATIONS for Foscar's funeral went on through the night. A wooden structure, made up of tied fagots dragged in from the woodland, grew taller beyond the big tribal camp. The constant crooning wail of the women in the tents produced a minor murmur of sound, enough to drive a man to the edge of madness. Ross had been left under guard where he could watch it all, a refinement of torture which he would earlier have believed too subtle for Ennar. Though the older men carried minor commands among the horsemen, because Ennar was the closest of blood kin among the adult males, he was in charge of the coming ceremony.

The pick of the horse herd, a roan stallion, was brought in to be picketed near Ross as sacrifice number two, and two of the hounds were in turn leashed close by. Foscar, his best weapons to hand and a red cloak lapped about him, lay waiting on a bier. Near-by squatted the tribal wizard, shaking his thunder rattle and chanting in a voice which ap-

proached a shriek. This wild activity might have been
a scene lifted directly from some tape stored at the
project base. It was very difficult for Ross to remember that this was reality, that he was to be one of
the main actors in the coming event, with no timely
aid from Operation Retrograde to snatch him to safety.

Sometime during that nightmare he slept, his
weariness of body overcoming him. He awoke, dazed,
to find a hand clutching his mop of hair, pulling his
head up.

"You sleep—you do not fear, Foscar's dog-one?"

Groggily Ross blinked up. Fear? Sure, he was
afraid. Fear, he realized with a clear thrust of consciousness such as he had seldom experienced before,
had always stalked beside him, slept in his bed. But he
had never surrendered to it, and he would not now if
he could help it.

"I do not fear!" He threw that creed into Ennar's
face in one hot boast. He *would* not fear!

"We shall see if you speak so loudly when the fire
bites you!" The other spat, yet in that oath there was
a reluctant recognition of Ross's courage.

"When the fire bites . . ." That sang in Ross's head.
There was something else—if he could only remember! Up to that moment he had kept a poor little
shadow of hope. It is always impossible—he was conscious again with that strange clarity of mind—for a
man to face his own death honestly. A man always
continues to believe to the last moment of his life that
something will intervene to save him.

The men led the horse to the mound of fagots
which was now crowned with Foscar's bier. The
stallion went quietly, until a tall tribesman struck true
with an ax, and the animal fell. The hounds were also

killed and laid at their dead master's feet.

But Ross was not to fare so easily. The wizard danced about him, a hideous figure in a beast mask, a curled fringe of dried snakeskins swaying from his belt. Shaking his rattle, he squawked like an angry cat as they pulled Ross to the stacked wood.

Fire—there was something about fire—if he could only remember! Ross stumbled and nearly fell across one leg of the dead horse they were propping into place. Then he remembered that tongue of flame in the meadow grass which had burned the horse but not the rider. His hands and his head would have no protection, but the rest of his body was covered with the flame-resistant fabric of the alien suit. Could he do it? There was such a slight chance, and they were already pushing him onto the mound, his hands tied. Ennar stooped, and bound his ankles, securing him to the brush.

So fastened, they left him. The tribe ringed around the pyre at a safe distance, Ennar and five other men approaching from different directions, torches aflame. Ross watched those blazing knots thrust into the brush and heard the crackle of the fire. His eyes, hard and measuring, studied the flash of flame from dried brush to seasoned wood.

A tongue of yellow-red flame licked up at him. Ross hardly dared to breathe as it wreathed about his foot, his hide fetters smoldering. The insulation of the suit did not cut all the heat, but it allowed him to stay put for the few seconds he needed to make his escape spectacular.

The flame had eaten through his foot bonds, and yet the burning sensation on his feet and legs was no greater than it would have been from the direct rays of a bright summer sun. Ross moistened his lips with his tongue. The impact of heat on his hands and face was different. He leaned down, held his wrists to the flame, taking in stoical silence the burns which freed him.

Then, as the fire curled up so that he seemed to stand in a frame of writhing red banners, Ross leaped through that curtain, protecting his bowed head with his arms as best he could. But to the onlookers it seemed he passed unhurt through the heart of a roaring fire.

He kept his footing and stood facing that part of the tribal ring directly before him. He heard a cry, perhaps of fear, and a blazing torch flew through the air and struck his hip. Although he felt the force of the blow, the burning bits of the head merely slid down his thigh and leg, leaving no mark on the smooth blue fabric.

"Ahhhhhhh!"

Now the wizard capered before him, shaking his rattle to make a deafening din. Ross struck out, slapping the sorcerer out of his path, and stooped to pick up the smoldering brand which had been thrown at him. Whirling it about his head, though every movement was torture to his scorched hands, he set it flaming once more. Holding it in front of him as a weapon, he stalked directly at the men and women before him.

The torch was a poor enough defense against spears and axes, but Ross did not care—he put into this last gamble all the determination he could summon. Nor did he realize what a figure he presented to the tribesmen. A man who had crossed a curtain of fire without apparent hurt, who appeared to wash in tongues of flame without harm, and who now called upon fire in turn as a weapon, was no man but a demon!

The wall of people wavered and broke. Women screamed and ran; men shouted. But no one threw a spear or struck with an ax. Ross walked on, a man possessed, looking neither to the right or left. He was in the camp now, stalking toward the fire burning before Foscar's tent. He did not turn aside for that either, but holding the torch high, strode through the heart of the flames, risking further burns for the sake of insuring his ultimate safety.

The tribesmen melted away as he approached the last line of tents, with the open land beyond. The horses of the herd, which had been driven to this side to avoid the funeral pyre, were shifting nervously, the scent of burning making them uneasy.

Once more Ross whirled the dying torch about his head. Recalling how the aliens had sent his horse mad, he tossed it behind him into the grass between the tents and the herd. The tinder-dry stuff caught immediately. Now if the men tried to ride after him, they would have trouble.

Without hindrance he walked across the meadow at the same even pace, never turning to look behind. His hands were two separate worlds of smarting pain; his hair and eyebrows were singed, and a finger of burn ran along the angle of his jaw. But he was free, and he did not believe that Foscar's men would be in any haste to pursue him. Somewhere before him lay the river, the river which ran to the sea. Ross walked on in the sunny morning while behind him black smoke raised a dark beacon to the sky.

Afterward he guessed that he must have been light-headed for several days, remembering little save the pain in his hands and the fact that it was necessary to keep moving. Once he fell to his knees and buried both hands in the cool, moist earth where a thread of stream trickled from a pool. The muck seemed to

draw out a little of the agony while he drank with a
fever thirst.

Ross seemed to move through a haze which lifted
at intervals during which he noted his surroundings,
was able to recall a little of what lay behind him, and
to keep to the correct route. However, the gaps of
time in between were forever lost to him. He stumbled
along the banks of a river and fronted a bear fishing.
The massive beast rose on its hind legs, growled, and
Ross walked by it uncaring, unmenaced by the
puzzled animal.

Sometimes he slept through the dark periods which
marked the nights, or he stumbled along under the
moon, nursing his hands against his breast, whimper-
ing a little when his foot slipped and the jar of that
mishap ran through his body. Once he heard singing,
only to realize that it was himself who sang hoarsely
a melody which would be popular thousands of years
later in the world through which he wavered. But
always Ross knew that he must go on, using that
thick stream of running water as a guide to his final
goal, the sea.

After a long while those spaces of mental clarity
grew longer, appearing closer together. He dug small
shelled things from under stones along the river and
ate them avidly. Once he clubbed a rabbit and
feasted. He sucked birds' eggs from a nest hidden
among some reeds—just enough to keep his gaunt
body going, though his gray eyes were now set in
what was almost a death's-head.

Ross did not know just when he realized that he
was again being hunted. It started with an uneasiness
which differed from his previous fever-bred hallu-
cinations. This was an inner pulling, a growing compulsion to turn and retrace his way back toward the

mountains to meet something, or someone, waiting for him on the backward path.

But Ross kept on, fearing sleep now and fighting it. For once he had lain down to rest and had wakened on his feet, heading back as if that compulsion had the power to take over his body when his waking will was off guard.

So he rested, but he dared not sleep, the desire constantly tearing at his will, striving to take over his weakened body and draw it back. Perhaps against all reason he believed that it was the aliens who were trying to control him. Ross did not even venture to guess why they were so determined to get him. If there were tribesmen on his trail as well, he did not know, but he was sure that this was now purely a war of wills.

As the banks of the river were giving way to marshes, he had to wade through mud and water, detouring the boggy sections. Great clouds of birds whirled and shrieked their protests at his coming, and sleek water animals paddled and poked curious heads out of the water as this two-legged thing walked mechanically through their green land. Always that pull was with him, until Ross was more aware of fighting it than of traveling.

Why did they want him to return? Why did they not follow him? Or were they afraid to venture too far from where they had come through the transfer? Yet the unseen rope which was tugging at him did not grow less tenuous as he put more distance between himself and the mountain valley. Ross could understand neither their motives nor their methods, but he could continue to fight.

The bog was endless. He found an island and lashed himself with his suit belt to the single willow which grew there, knowing that he must have sleep, or he could not hope to last through the next day. Then he slept, only to waken cold, shaking, and afraid. Shoulder deep in a pool, he was aware that in his sleep he must have opened the belt buckle and freed himself, and only the mishap of falling into the water had brought him around to sanity.

Somehow he got back to the tree, rehooked the buckle and twisted the belt around the branches so that he was sure he could not work it free until daybreak. He lapsed into a deepening doze, and awoke, still safely anchored, with the morning cries of the birds. Ross considered the suit as he untangled the belt. Could the strange clothing be the tie by which the aliens held to him? If he were to strip, leaving the garment behind, would he be safe?

He tried to force open the studs across his chest, but they would not yield to the slight pressure which was all his seared fingers could exert, and when he pulled at the fabric, he was unable to tear it. So, still wearing the livery of the off-world men, Ross continued on his way, hardly caring where he went or how. The mud plastered on him by his frequent falls was some protection against the swarm of insect life his passing stirred into attack. However, he was able to endure a swollen face and slitted eyes, being far more conscious of the wrenching feeling within him than the misery of his body.

The character of the marsh began to change once more. The river was splitting into a dozen smaller streams, shaping out fanlike. Looking down at this from one of the marsh hillocks, Ross knew a faint surge of relief. Such a place had been on the map Ashe had made them memorize. He was close to the sea at last, and for the moment that was enough.

A salt-sharpened wind cut at him with the force of a fist in the face. In the absence of sunlight the leaden clouds overhead set a winterlike gloom across the countryside. To the constant sound of birdcalls Ross tramped heavily through small pools, beating a path through tangles of marsh grass. He stole eggs from nests, sucking his nourishment eagerly with no dislike for the fishy flavor, and drinking from stagnant, brackish ponds.

Suddenly Ross halted, at first thinking that the continuous roll of sound he heard was thunder. Yet the clouds overhead were massed no more than before and there was no sign of lightning. Continuing on, he realized that the mysterious sound was the pounding of surf—he was near the sea!

Willing his body to run, he weaved forward at a reeling trot, pitting all his energy against the incessant pull from behind. His feet skidded out of marsh mud into sand. Ahead of him were dark rocks surrounded by the white lace of spray.

Ross headed straight toward that spray until he stood knee-deep in the curling, foam-edged water and felt its tug on his body almost as strong as that other tug upon his mind. He knelt, letting the salt water sting to life every cut, every burn, sputtering as it filled his mouth and nostrils, washing from him the slime of the bog lands. It was cold and bitter, but it was the sea! He had made it!

Ross Murdock staggered back and sat down suddenly in the sand. Glancing about, he saw that his refuge was a rough triangle between two of the small river arms, littered with the debris of the spring floods which had grounded here after rejection by the sea.

Although there was plenty of material for a fire, he had no means of kindling a flame, having lost the flint all Beaker traders carried for such a purpose.

This was the sea, and against all odds he had reached it. He lay back, his self-confidence restored to the point where he dared once more to consider the future. He watched the swooping flight of gulls drawing patterns under the clouds above. For the moment he wanted nothing more than to lie here and rest.

But he did not surrender to this first demand of his overdriven body for long. Hungry and cold, sure that a storm was coming, he knew he had to build a fire—a fire on shore could provide him with the means of signaling the sub. Hardly knowing why—because one part of the coastline was as good as another—Ross began to walk again, threading a path in and out among the rocky outcrops.

So he found it, a hollow between two such windbreaks within which was a blackened circle of small stones holding charred wood, with some empty shells piled near-by. Here was unmistakable evidence of a camp! Ross plunged forward, thrusting a hand impetuously into the black mass of the dead fire. To his astonishment, he touched warmth!

Hardly daring to disturb those precious bits of charcoal, he dug around them, then carefully blew into what appeared to be dead ashes. There was an answering glow! He could not have just imagined it.

From a pile of wood that had been left behind, Ross snatched a small twig, poking it at the coal after he had rubbed it into a brush on the rough rock. He watched, all one ache of hope. The twig caught!

With his stiff fingers so clumsy, he had to be very careful, but Ross had learned patience in a hard school. Bit by bit he fed that tiny blaze until he had a real fire. Then, leaning back back against the rock, he watched it.

It was now obvious that the placement of the original fire had been chosen with care, for the outcrops gave it wind shelter. They also provided a dark backdrop, partially hiding the flames on the landward side but undoubtedly making them more visible from the sea. The site seemed just right for a signal fire—but to what?

Ross's hands shook slightly as he fed the blaze. It was only too clear why anyone would make a signal on this shore. McNeil—or perhaps both he and Ashe —had survived the breakup of the raft, after all. They had reached this point—abandoned no earlier than this morning, judging by the life remaining in the coals—and put up the signal. Then, just as arranged, they had been collected by the sub, by now on its way back to the hidden North American post. There was no hope of any pickup for him now. Just as he had believed them dead after he had found that rag on the sapling, so they must have thought him finished after his fall in the river. He was just a few hours too late!

Ross folded his arms across his hunched knees and rested his head on them. There was no possible way he could ever reach the post or his own kind—ever again. Thousands of miles lay between him and the temporary installation in this time.

He was so sunk in his own complete despair that he was long unaware of finally being free of the pressure to turn back which had so long haunted him. But as he roused to feed the fire he got to wondering. Had those who hunted him given up the chase? Since he had lost his own race with time, he did not really care. What did it matter?

The pile of wood was getting low, but he decided

that did not matter either. Even so, Ross got to his feet, moving over to the drifts of storm wrack to gather more. Why should he stay here by a useless beacon? But somehow he could not force himself to move on, as futile as his vigil seemed.

Dragging the sun-dried, bleached limbs of long-dead trees to his half shelter, he piled them up, working until he laughed at the barricade he had built. "A siege!" For the first time in days he spoke aloud. "I might be ready for a siege . . ." He pulled over another branch, added it to his pile, and kneeled down once more by the flames.

There were fisherfolk to be found along this coast, and tomorrow when he was rested he would strike south and try to find one of their primitive villages. Traders would be coming into this territory now that the Red-inspired raiders were gone. If he could contact them . . .

But that spark of interest in the future died almost as soon as it was born. To be a Beaker trader as an agent for the project was one thing, to live the role for the rest of his life was something else.

Ross stood by his fire, staring out to sea for a sign he knew he would never see again as long as he lived. Then, as if a spear had struck between his shoulder blades, he was attacked.

The blow was not physical, but came instead as a tearing, red pain in his head, a pressure so terrible he could not move. He knew instantly that behind him now lurked the ultimate danger.

18

Ross FOUGHT to break that hold, to turn his head, to face the peril which crept upon him now. Unlike anything he had ever met before in his short lifetime, it could only have come from some alien source. This strange encounter was a battle of will against will! The same rebellion against authority which had ruled his boyhood, which had pushed him into the orbit of the project, stiffened him to meet this attack.

He was going to turn his head; he was going to see who stood there. He *was!* Inch by inch, Ross's head came around, though sweat stung his seared and bitten flesh, and every breath was an effort. He caught a half glimpse of the beach behind the rocks, and the stretch of sand was empty. Overhead the birds were gone—as if they had never existed. Or, as if they had been swept away by some impatient fighter, who wanted no distractions from the purpose at hand.

Having successfully turned his head, Ross decided to turn his body. His left hand went out, slowly, as if it moved some great weight. His palm gritted painfully on the rock and he savored that pain, for it pierced through the dead blanket of compulsion that was being used against him. Deliberately he ground his blistered skin against the stone, concentrating on the sharp torment in his hand as the agony shot up his arm. While he focused his attention on the physical pain, he could feel the pressure against him weaken. Summoning all his strength, Ross swung around in a movement which was only a shadow of his former feline grace.

The beach was still empty, except for the piles of driftwood, the rocks, and the other things he had originally found there. Yet he knew that something was waiting to pounce. Having discovered that for him pain was a defense weapon, he had that one resource. If they took him, it would be after besting him in a fight.

Even as he made this decision, Ross was conscious of a curious weakening of the force bent upon him. It was as if his opponents had been surprised, either at his simple actions of the past few seconds or at his determination. Ross leaped upon that surprise, adding it to his stock of unseen weapons.

He leaned forward, still grinding his torn hand against the rock as a steadying influence, took up a length of dried wood, and thrust its end into the fire. Having once used fire to save himself, he was ready and willing to do it again, although at the same time, another part of him shrank from what he intended.

Holding his improvised torch breast-high, Ross stared across it, searching the land for the faintest sign of his enemies. In spite of the fire and the light he held before him, the dusk prevented him from seeing too far. Behind him the crash of the surf could have covered the noise of a marching army.

"Come and get me!"

He whirled his brand into bursting life and then hurled it straight into the drift among the dunes. He was grabbing for a second brand almost before the blazing head of the first had fallen into the twisted, bleached roots of a dead tree.

He stood tense, a second torch now kindled in his hand. The sharp vise of another's will which had nipped him so tightly a moment ago was easing, slowly disappearing as water might trickle away. Yet he could not believe that this small act of defiance had so daunted his unseen opponent as to make him give up the struggle this easily. It was more likely the pause of a wrestler seeking for a deadlier grip.

The brand in his hand—Ross's second line of defense—was a weapon he was loath to use, but would use if he were forced to it. He kept his hand mercilessly flat against the rock as a reminder and a spur.

Fire twisted and crackled among the driftwood where the first torch had lodged, providing a flickering light yards from where he stood. He was grateful for it in the gloom of the gathering storm. If they would only come to open war before the rain struck . . .

Ross sheltered his torch with his body as spray, driven inward from the sea, spattered his shoulders and his back. If it rained, he would lose what small advantage the fire gave him, but then he would find some other way to meet them. They would neither break him nor take him, even if he had to wade into the sea and swim out into the lash of the cold northern waves until he could not move his tired limbs any longer.

Once again that steel-edge will struck at Ross, probing his stubbornness, assaulting his mind. He whirled the torch, brought the scorching breath of the flame across the hand resting on the rock. Unable to control his own cry of protest, he was not sure he had the fortitude to repeat such an act.

He had won again! The pressure had fallen away in a flick, almost as if some current had been snapped off. Through the red curtain of his torment Ross sensed a surprise and disbelief. He was unaware that in this queer duel he was using both a power of will and a depth of perception he had never known he possessed. Because of his daring, he had shaken his opponents as no physical attack could have affected them.

"Come and get me!" He shouted again at the barren shoreline where the fire ate at the drift and nothing stirred, yet something very much alive and conscious lay hidden. This time there was more than simple challenge in Ross's demand—there was a note of triumph.

The spray whipped by him, striking at his fire, at the brand he held. Let the sea water put both out! He would find another way of fighting. He was certain of that, and he sensed that those out there knew it too and were troubled.

The fire was being driven by the wind along the crisscross lines of bone-white wood left high on the beach, forming a wall of flame between him and the interior, not, however, an insurmountable barrier to whatever lurked there.

Again Ross leaned against the rock, studying the length of beach. Had he been wrong in thinking that they were within the range of his voice? The power they had used might carry over a greater distance.

"Yahhhh—" Instead of a demand, he now voiced a taunting cry, screaming his defiance. Some wild madness had been transmitted to him by the winds, the roaring sea, his own pain. Ready to face the worst they could send against him, he tried to hurl that thought back at them as they had struck with their united will at him. No answer came to his challenge, no rise to counter-attack.

Moving away from the rock, Ross began to walk forward toward the burning drift, his torch ready in his hand. "I am here!" he shouted into the wind. "Come out—face me!"

It was then that he saw those who had tracked him. Two tall thin figures, wearing dark clothes, were standing quietly watching him, their eyes dark holes in the white ovals of their faces.

Ross halted. Though they were separated by yards of sand and rock and a burning barrier, he could feel the force they wielded. The nature of that force had changed, however. Once it had struck with a vigorous spear point; now it formed a shield of protection. Ross could not break through that shield, and they dared not drop it. A stalemate existed between them in this strange battle, the like of which Ross's world had not known before.

He watched those expressionless white faces, trying to find some reply to the deadlock. There flashed into his mind the certainty that while he lived and moved, and they lived and moved, this struggle, this unending pursuit, would continue. For some mysterious reason they wanted to have him under their control, but that was never going to happen if they all had to remain here on this strip of water-washed sand until they starved to death! Ross tried to drive that thought across to them.

"Murrrrdock!" That croaking cry borne out of the sea by the wind might almost have come from the bill of a sea bird.

"Murrrrdock!"

Ross spun around. Visibility had been drastically curtailed by the lowering clouds and the dashing spray, but he could see a round dark thing bobbing on the waves. The sub? A raft?

Sensing a movement behind him, Ross wheeled about as one of the alien figures leaped the blazing drift, heedless of the flames, and ran light-footedly toward him in what could only be an all-out attempt at capture. The man had ready a weapon like the one that had felled Foscar. Ross threw himself at his opponent in a reckless dive, falling on him with a smashing impact.

In Ross's grasp the alien's body was fragile, but he moved fluidly as Murdock fought to break his grip on the hand weapon and pin him to the sand. Ross was too intent upon his own part of the struggle to heed the sounds of a shot over his head and a thin, wailing cry. He slammed his opponent's hand against a stone, and the white face, inches away from his own, twisted silently with pain.

Fumbling for a better hold, Ross was sent rolling. He came down on his left hand with a force which brought tears to his eyes and stopped him just long enough for the other to regain his feet.

The blue-suited man sprinted back to the body of his fellow where it lay by the drift. He slung his unconscious comrade over the barrier with more ease than Ross would have believed possible and vaulted the barrier after him. Ross, half crouched on the sand, felt unusually light and empty. The strange tie which had drawn and held him to the strangers had been broken.

"Murdock!"

A rubber raft rode in on the waves, two men

aboard it. Ross got up, pulling at the studs of his suit with his right hand. He could believe in what he saw now—the sub had not left, after all. The two men running toward him through the dusk were of his own kind.

"Murdock!"

It did not seem at all strange that Kelgarries reached him first. Ross, caught up in this dream, appealed to the major for aid with the studs. If the strangers from the ship did trace him by the suit, they were not going to follow the sub back to the post and serve the project as they had the Reds.

"Got—to—get—this—off—" He pulled the words out one by one, tugging frantically at the stubborn studs. "They can trace this and follow us—"

Kelgarries needed no better explanation. Ripping loose the fastenings, he pulled the clinging fabric from Ross, sending him reeling with pain as he pulled the left sleeve down the younger man's arm.

The wind and spray were ice on his body as they dragged him down to the raft, bundling him aboard. He did not at all remember their arrival on board the sub. He was lying in the vibrating heart of the undersea ship when he opened his eyes to see Kelgarries regarding him intently. Ashe, a coat of bandage about his shoulder and chest, lay on a neighboring bunk. McNeil stood watching a medical corpsman lay out supplies.

"He needs a shot," the medic was saying as Ross blinked at the major.

"You left the suit—back there?" Ross demanded.

"We did. What's this about them tracing you by it? Who was tracing you?"

"Men from the space ship. That's the only way they

could have trailed me down the river." He was finding it difficult to talk, and the protesting medic kept waving a needle in his direction, but somehow in bursts of half-finished sentences Ross got out his story—Foscar's death, his own escape from the chief's funeral pyre, and the weird duel of wills back on the beach. Even as he poured it out he thought how unlikely most of it must sound. Yet Kelgarries appeared to accept every word, and there was no expression of disbelief on Ashe's face.

"So that's how you got those burns," said the major slowly when Ross had finished his story. "Deliberately searing your hand in the fire to break their hold—" He crashed his fist against the wall of the tiny cabin and then, when Ross winced at the jar, he hurriedly uncurled those fingers to press Ross's shoulder with a surprisingly warm and gentle touch. "Put him to sleep," he ordered the medic. "He deserves about a month of it, I should judge. I think he has brought us a bigger slice of the future than we had hoped for . . ."

Ross felt the prick of the needle and then nothing more. Even when he was carried ashore at the post and later when he was transported into his proper time, he did not awaken. He only approached a strange dreamy state in which he ate and drowsed, not caring for the world beyond his own bunk.

But there came a day when he did care, sitting up to demand food with a great deal of his old self-assertion. The doctor looked him over, permitting him to get out of bed and try out his legs. They were exceedingly uncooperative at first, and Ross was glad he had tried to move only from his bunk to a waiting chair.

"Visitors welcome?"

Ross looked up eagerly and then smiled, somewhat hesitatingly, at Ashe. The older man wore his arm in a sling but otherwise seemed his usual imperturbable self.

"Ashe, tell me what happened. Are we back at the main base? What about the Reds? We weren't traced by the ship people, were we?"

Ashe laughed. "Did Doc just wind you up to let you spin, Ross? Yes, this is home, sweet home. As for the rest—well, it is a long story, and we are still picking up pieces of it here and there."

Ross pointed to the bunk in invitation. "Can you tell me what is known?" He was still somewhat at a loss, his old secret awe of Ashe tempering his outward show of eagerness. Ross still feared one of those snubs the other so well knew how to deliver to the bumptious. But Ashe did come in and sit down, none of his old formality now in evidence.

"You have been a surprise package, Murdock." His observation had some of the ring of the old Ashe, but there was no withdrawal behind the words. "Rather a busy lad, weren't you, after you were bumped off into that river?"

Ross's reply was a grimace. "You heard all about that!" He had no time for his own adventures, already receding into a past which made them both dim and unimportant. "What happened to you—and to the project—and—"

"One thing at a time, and don't rush your fences." Ashe was surveying him with an odd intentness which Ross could not understand. He continued to explain in his "instructor" voice. "We made it down the river —how, don't ask me. That was something of a 'project' in itself," he laughed. "The raft came apart piece by piece, and we waded most of the last couple of miles, I think. I'm none too clear on the details; you'll have to get those out of McNeil, who was still among those present then. Other than that, we cannot compete with your adventures. We built a signal fire and sat by it toasting our shins for a few days, until the sub came to collect us—"

"And took you off." Ross experienced a fleeting return of that hollow feeling he had known on the shore when the still-warm coals of the signal fire had told him the story of his too-late arrival.

"And took us off. But Kelgarries agreed to spin out our waiting period for another twenty-four hours, in case you did manage to survive that toss you took into the river. Then we sighted your spectacular display of fireworks on the beach, and the rest was easy."

"The ship people didn't trace us back to post?"

"Not that we know of. Anyway, we've closed down the post on that time level. You might be interested in a very peculiar tale our modern agents have picked up, floating over and under the iron curtain. A blast went off in the Baltic region of this time, wiping some installation clean off the map. The Reds have kept quiet as to the nature of the explosion and the exact place where it occurred."

"The aliens followed *them* all the way up to this time!"—Ross half rose from the chair—"But why? And why did they trail me?"

"That we can only guess. But I don't believe that they were moved by any private vengeance for the looting of their derelict. There is some more imperative reason why they don't want us to find or use anything from one of their cargoes—"

"But they were in power thousands of years ago. Maybe they and their worlds are gone now. Why should things we do today matter to them?"

"Well, it does matter, and in some very important way. And we have to learn that reason."

"How?" Ross looked down at his left hand, encased in a mitten of bandage under which he very gingerly tried to stretch a finger. Maybe he should have been eager to welcome another meeting with the ship people, but if he were truly honest, he had to admit that he did not. He glanced up, sure that Ashe had read all that hesitation and scorned him for it. But there was no sign that his discomfiture had been noticed.

"By doing some looting of our own," Ashe answered.

"Those tapes we brought back are going to be a big help. More than one derelict was located. We were right in our surmise that the Reds first discovered the remains of one in Siberia, but it was in no condition to be explored. They already had the basic idea of the time traveler, so they applied it to the hunting down of other ships, with several way stops to throw people like us off the scent. So they found an intact ship, and also several others. At least three are on *this* side of the Atlantic where they couldn't get at them very well. Those we can deal with now—"

"Won't the aliens be waiting for us to try that?"

"As far as we can discover they don't know where any of these ships crashed. Either there were no survivors, or passengers and crew took off in lifeboats while they were still in space. They might never have known of the Reds' activities if you hadn't triggered that communicator on the derelict."

Ross was reduced to a small boy who badly needed an alibi for some piece of juvenile mischief. "I didn't mean to." That excuse sounded so feeble that he was surprised into a laugh, only to see Ashe grinning back at him.

"Seeing as how your action also put a very effective spike in the opposition's wheel, you are freely forgiven. Anyway, you have also provided us with a pretty good idea of what we may be up against with the aliens, and we'll be prepared for that next time."

"Then there will be a next time?"

"We are calling in all time agents, concentrating our forces in the right period. Yes, there will be a next time. We have to learn just what they are trying so hard to protect."

"What do you think it is?"

"Space!" Ashe spoke the word softly as if he relished the promise it held.

"Space?"

"That ship you explored was a derelict from a galactic fleet, but it was a ship and it used the principle of space flight. Do you understand now? In these lost ships lies the secret which will make us free of all the stars! We must claim it."

"Can we—?"

"Can *we?*" Ashe was laughing at Ross again with his eyes, though his face remained sober. "Then *you* still want to be counted in on this game?"

Ross looked down again at his bandaged hand and remembered swiftly so many things—the coast of Britain on a misty morning, the excitement of prowling the alien ship, the fight with Ennar, even the long nightmare of his flight down the river, and lastly, the exultation he had tasted when he had faced the alien and had locked wills—to hold steady. He knew that he could not, would not, give up what he had found here in the service of the project as long as it was in his power to cling to it.

"Yes." It was a very simple answer, but when his eyes met Ashe's, Ross knew that it would serve better than any solemn oath.